The Complete Irish Tinwhist
by
L.E. McCullough

Oak Publications
New York/London/Sydney

Musical notation by Susan Harger
Elf drawings by Dolores Heagy
Tinwhistle drawings by Bruce Berman
Titles by Patti O'Toole
Photo of L.E. McCollough by James Crary
Photo of Ron & Rico by Robert Higbie

First published and Copyright © 1976 by Silver Spear Publications.
This editon published and Copyright © 1987 by Oak Publications,
A Division of Music Sales Corporation, New York, NY.

Order No. OK 64923
US International Standard Book Number 0.8256.0311.0
UK International Standard Book Number 0.7119.1448.6

Exclusive Distributors:
Music Sales Corporation
257 Park Avenue South, New York, NY 10010, USA
Music Sales Limited
8/9 Frith Street, London W1V 5TZ England
Music Sales Pty. Limited
120 Rothschild Street, Rosebery, Sydney, NSW 2018, Australia

Printed in the United States of America by
Vicks Lithograph and Printing Corporation

CONTENTS

FOREWORD

In offering this book to the public I make no apologies, nor do I labor under any delusions of omniscience in the realm of Irish music. This book is the result of being continually asked by persons who have just purchased a tinwhistle, "Where can I learn to play?" Aside from a handful of Irish music schools in a few major American cities, there is no formal source of instruction for the tinwhistle. Yet, Irish music is difficult to pick up without any assistance, and it is an established fact that many new enthusiasts live impossibly far from Irish tinwhistle players or from any Irish musicians at all. While there are increasing numbers of actual and forthcoming tutors on the market, their availibility is often limited, and, indeed, the scope and content of these tutors is also not infrequently limited in various ways. There remains a definite need for a complete, systematic, accessible work on the tinwhistle in which the full potential of the instrument is thoroughly explored and comprehensibly explained. That, in a paragraph, is why this book has been written.

This book assumes a basic reading knowledge of standard Western music notation in the treble clef, and a few introductory remarks about Irish music have been included for those coming to the music anew. Readers unfamiliar with musical notation should not feel that they are irremediably beyond hope. It's not hard to learn, and it's a proven method of musical shorthand that helps the learning process to a high degree. Contrary to popular misconception, most Irish musicians know how to read and write music, and they aren't any the less traditional or authentic because of it.

By the end of the first instructional section, you should be able to dig into the tunes that follow. Over the past four years since the tutor was first issued, I have received many comments that the tunes in the back of the book were too difficult. Sorry, Jim, but all you have to do is keep looking through until you find an easy one. The tunes are still arranged according to the type of tune, simply because that's the way editors of Irish music collections have been organizing their work for three centuries; it's a sensible method, too. So when you're ready to start playing the tunes in the back, you could start with an air, or one of the harp tunes, or perhaps a polka or slide. As you feel more comfortable with the music, then attempt tunes that are more ornamented and challenging. These tunes represent a cross-section of Irish music and are presented in versions especially suited to the tinwhistle. Since this book was first published, many of these tunes have been recorded, and so you will be able to locate variant settings to add to the ones given here.

The revisions in this edition consist of a few clarifications and elaborations of some points in the instructional section that should be of help to readers unacquainted with wind instruments or who have had an abbreviated musical background. More tablatures (a very useful system pioneered with this book and now imitated by other tinwhistle tutors), some drawings, two new tunes, an expanded and updated discography, some new information in the historical chapter and tune notes make up the rest of the additions—most of them inserted simply to satisfy the author's vain, unexpungeable desire for perfection rather than out of any dire necessity. The bulk of the book has remained unchanged because, judging from readers' responses since 1976, the tutor appears to be successfully serving its original purpose of communicating the fundamentals of Irish music performance on the tinwhistle. Hopefully, we've all had a good time doing it, too.

I could not finish this foreword without expressing my immense gratitude to the many musicians from whom I have learned virtually everything I know about Irish music. In particular I wish to thank fiddler Miles Krassen whose integrity, perseverance, and wisdom have proven continuously inspirational, and flute players Noel Rice and Seamus Cooley for teaching me rolls. Without their assistance and encouragement (as well as many others) this book could never have been written. To paraphrase the venerable Francis O'Neill, the great collector and chronicler of Irish music in 19th-century America:

"This book is respectfully dedicated to the multitude
of musicians of all races all over the world who
enjoy and cherish the Melodies of Ireland"

L.E. McCullough
Pittsburgh, Pa.   June 27,1980

Two whistleheads: Ron & Rico

2

SOME REMARKS ON IRISH MUSIC

Most of the music with which this book is concerned assumed its present form in the 18th century. It is not possible to pinpoint precisely the persons, places, or moments of genesis, as the music was (and is still) chiefly transmitted without the use of written notation. Also, Irish music was the creation of a rural peasantry that did not possess the means or probably even the desire to document the rise and spread of their music. Few of the persons who composed the tunes have ever been positively identified, and one can only conclude that the bulk of Irish music is the product of thousands of anonymous folk musicians scattered across the Irish countryside.

Irish music did not arise in a vacuum, however. Several of the slow airs and harp tunes in the current repertoire were undoubtedly composed by taking already existing pieces of music and reworking them—changing the meter and rhythm, reshaping the melodic structure, altering the tonality, adding new sections and deleting others. The 18th century was a period of social upheaval and cultural transition in Ireland; with the collapse of the old Gaelic social order, the country was laid open to a wave of new influences in all areas of society, and Irish music naturally reflected the contemporary state of affairs. Scholars have presented convincing evidence showing that the reel is derived from Scotland and the jig and hornpipe from England; indeed, a number of Scots and English tunes are still found in the current repertoire. The professional travelling dancing masters who flourished in 18th-century Ireland also had a part in the creation of new tune genres, as new dance patterns required new (or at least rearranged) dance accompaniments. Whatever the original sources of the various musical forms, the great majority of individual pieces in the tradition were composed by Irish fiddlers, pipers, flute and tinwhistle players in the 18th and early 19th centuries. The fact that new tunes are still being composed by Irish musicians working within the established traditional framework demonstrates the stability and vitality of the idiom, as well as its capacity to adapt to changing social contexts.

Irish music is fundamentally a tradition of solo performance in which the melodic line is of paramount importance. Though Irish music is often performed by more than one instrument and is frequently provided with harmonic and percussive accompaniment, a performance of a tune by a single musician is an entity complete in itself. Over the last decade new experiments in the ensemble performance of Irish music have had a noticeable impact on the tradition by promoting new tunes, tune settings, and styles, and by serving as a vehicle for acquainting the general public with Irish music. Despite the recent interest in the innovative possibilities inherent in the ensemble arrangement of Irish music and song, the solo musician and singer remain the essence of the tradition.

Irish music is, however, a developing tradition in both performance practice and instrumentation. The fiddle, uileann pipes, and various flutes, fifes, and tinwhistles were the instruments most commonly played until the middle of the 19th century. At that point the family of free-reed instruments began entering the idiom. Today this instrument species is represented in Irish music by the concertina, mouth organ, button and piano accordion, and a few melodeons still used mostly by older musicians. The latter part of the 19th century is also the period when the practice of harmonic accompaniment is believed to have started gaining favor, first with the piano and later with the guitar and other plectrum instruments. This development indicated the ability of the music to absorb urban, "modern" influences without being submerged or obliterated; the preference for harmonic accompaniment may well have originated in America, where Irish musicians were a staple element of minstrelsy, musical theater, and vaudeville during the 19th century. Though plectrum instruments such as the guitar, tenor banjo, and mandolin were being played by Irish musicians in the late 1800s, it is in only the last few years that they have truly achieved prominence in Irish music. The last two decades have also seen a revival of interest in the Irish harp, bones, and bodhran—ancient Irish instruments that have received an enthusiastic acceptance from 20th century aficianados.

Irish music consists chiefly of dance tunes and airs, though there are some pieces of music that are neither danced to nor used as airs for song texts—marches, tunes composed by harpers of the 17th and 18th centuries for aristo-cratic patrons, and descriptive pieces that depict a scene or event from Irish life or history. There were also at one time a handful of double jigs played "the piece way", that is, in a slow, highly embellished and elaborated form (see piper Pat Mitchell's Topic LP for a current example). It is the dance music that has dominated the repertoires of most Irish musicians during this century, despite the fact that Irish music and dance have followed their own separate paths of development since the 19th century.

The reel has become the most popular of the dance tune genres, though 18th and 19th century collections suggest that the double jig was the favorite tune type of that era. Present-day composers of Irish music seem to choose the reel as the primary vehicle for their inspiration, and it is not uncommon to attend sessions where nothing but reels will be played for extended periods of time. The single jig, like the double jig, is in 6/8 (though sometimes noted in 12/8) but differs slightly in its rhythmic emphasis and in the steps danced to it. In the province of Munster single jig tunes called slides have remained very popular and are generally written in 12/8 time. The slip or hop jig is in 9/8, the only one of the 18th-century solo dances to be performed in triple meter. Hornpipes, like reels, are in 4/4 but are played with more deliberate emphasis on the strong beats of each measure so that the first and third beats are like dotted eighth notes. Set dances, also called long dances, were devised by the dancing masters as the ultimate showcase for their terpsichorean skills, and each set dance is performed to its own special tune. These tunes are either in 6/8 or 4/4 time and have extended second parts twelve or more bars long. The majority of dance tunes consist of two eight-measure sections, though some tunes have three or more parts and may vary in the order and number of times each part is repeated.

Most of the music used to accompany the numerous ensemble dances popular in Ireland during the 18th century appears to have been fairly indigenous. During the early 19th century, the dancing masters introduced group dances adapted from the quadrilles then popular on the Continent. Known as "sets" (or "half-sets" if two instead of four couples danced) these dances were in 6/8 and 2/4 time

4

and made use of simple jigs and reels then extant. Several of these set tunes survive today in the guise of slides and polkas. Later in the 19th century, schottisches, highland flings, polkas, waltzes, barn dances, mazurkas, quicksteps, and varsoviennes emigrated to Ireland from European ballrooms and were naturalized into the Irish tradition. Again, the process of reworking existing tunes asserted itself, and much of the music used to accompany these dances has been drawn from native sources.

There has been some dispute among scholars regarding the classification of pieces of music known variously as "airs", "song airs", "slow airs", or "narrative airs". They are in most instances wedded (or were at one time) to lyrics in English and/or Irish. In some cases, only the airs have survived and have assumed a new identity of their own. To complicate the issue further, many Irish folk songs are often sung to dance tunes, especially jigs.

Currently, the most frequently played airs derive from the sean-nós ("old style" or "old manner") tradition of Gaelic singing. These airs are often called slow airs because of the slow performance tempo and the rubato method of interpretation in which the basic rhythmic structure of the air is varied according to the demands of the text and the creativity of the singer. The sean-nós style is also highly ornamented and, though reducible on paper to a fairly simple, symmetrical structure, often gives the impression of amorphousness to those hearing it for the first time.

To present a complete transcription of a slow air would be of little value except for purely illustrative or analytic purposes. Most players agree that the best way to learn a slow air is to listen to it being sung; in this way, all the nuances and expressive devices present in a virtuosic, soulful interpretation of a sean-nós performance can be absorbed. Often, however, it is only possible to learn an air from a musician, and, in this instance, it is perhaps a case of the spirit rather than the letter of the law being preserved, as the traditions of vocal and instrumental music are distinct, though related. The airs found in this book are not from the sean-nós tradition, though they can be enhanced by introducing sean-nós techniques of interpretation. Perhaps more than any other genre of Irish music, airs must remain in the living tradition to retain their genuine character and vibrancy.

For more details on Irish music, song, and dance, these books will be useful: Folk Music and Dances of Ireland, Breandán Breathnach (Talbot Press, Dublin, 1971); A Handbook of Irish Dances, J.G. O'Keeffe and Art O'Brien (Gill and MacMillan, Dublin, 1954); Songs of Irish Rebellion, Georges-Denis Zimmerman (Folklore Associates, Hatboro, Pennsylvania, 1967).

HISTORICAL NOTES ON THE TINWHISTLE

"Sweet as pipe-music was the melodious sound of the maiden's voice and her Gaelic"—Accalam na Senórach (The Colloquy of the Ancient Men), 12th century

"Pipes, fiddles, men of no valour, bone-players and pipe-players; a crowd hideous, noisy, profane, shriekers and shouters"—"The Fair of Carman" in The Book of Leinster, c. 1160 A.D.

The instrument now known among Irish musicians as the tinwhistle, penny-whistle, or tinflute, has a lengthy pedigree in the historical annals of Irish music. While the oldest surviving specimens are the 12th-century bone whistles recently unearthed at the High Street excavations in the old Norman quarter of Dublin, various types of whistle flutes that were the progenitors of the modern tinwhistle are frequently mentioned in the ancient tales and in the laws governing ancient Irish society. There is the tale in which Ailen, a chief of the fairy tribe Tuatha de Danann, uses the feadán to cast a spell of sleep over the inhabitants of the High King's palace at Tara, so that he can carry out his annual November Eve vengeance. Players of the feadán are also mentioned in the description of the King of Ireland's court found in the Brehon Laws dating from the 3rd century A.D. The 12th-century reference in the poem about the pre-Christian Fair of Carman includes cuisleannach (players of the cuisle, or pipe) among the entertainers, despite an obvious aesthetic disapproval on the poet's part. A more complimentary view of the cuisle is expressed by the 12th-century compiler of the Acallam na Senórach in the comparison of its timbre and the sound of a maiden's speech. One of the most interesting references occurs in an ancient poem found in the Teach Miodhchuarta where the seating plan of the royal feasts at Tara is given; cuisleannach are placed in the same division as smiths, shield-makers, jugglers, trumpeters, shoemakers, and fishermen, to name a few of their social compatriots. It might be of some interest to note that the cuisleannach received the pig's thigh as their allotted portion.

Through the efforts of 19th-century specialists in ancient Irish society, it has been possible to obtain some insight into the nature of the various "musical pipes" that flourished during this time. Both the feadán (also called feadóg) and cuisle (also called cuiseach) refer to a "pipe, tube, artery, vein" and were made by hollowing out the stalks of plants such as elder, cane, and other wild grasses and reeds (an additional meaning of feadán is "a hollowed stick"). Uileann pipemaker Patrick Hennelly of Chicago recalled that as a young lad in Mayo, he often made musical instruments from ripe oat straws simply by pushing out the pith and then fashioning the lip and fingerholes with a penknife, and, indeed, the basic structural principles of such instruments must have been discovered fairly early and by many people. Later, as the technology advanced, more permanent materials such as wood and bone came into use, and various fipples, tongues, and reeds were devised for sounding the instruments.

Stone high-crosses of the 9th, 10th, and 11th centuries reveal these pipes to have been straight or sometimes slightly curved up at the bottom. They possessed narrow conical bores that widened toward the bottom and are estimated to have been between 14 and 24 inches long. Currently-manufactured tinwhistles in the key of Bb (actually pitched two whole tones below concert pitch) measure 14 and 3/4 inches in length, but there is little reliable information about the scales or pitch resources of the feadán or cuisle. Possibly, harmonics or over-blown notes may have been used, as is the case with similar types of simple flutes throughout the world. End-blown pipes representative of the general type found in medieval Britain and Ireland were discovered in Somerset and Monmouth-shire, England. Made of deer bone, they each had five front fingerholes; one had two rear thumbholes, while the other pipe had one. One pipe had a range of 1½ octaves, the other 2½. These pipes were restored to playable condition, and it was found that each could give diatonic scales (as can the modern tinwhistle). It is not unlikely that a relatively sophisticated music was played on ancient bone pipes of this kind.

Occasionally, these pipes were depicted as being played in twos and threes by the same player; this might have been achieved by holding two or three different pipes in the hands, similar to the ancient Greek aulos and Roman tibia. In ancient times double reeds made of cane were used to sound the pipes. It is possible that the tubes were bound together like the parallel double and triple pipes still found in Eastern and Southern Europe and North Africa. In any case, the possibility exists that harmonies and countermelodies may have been practiced by players of the feadán and cuisle.

There is some difference of opinion concerning the instrument known as the buinne (or bunne). Some scholars believe it was a horn or trumpet used for military and hunting purposes rather than general musical entertainment, while others think it was similar to the feadán and cuisle and was equipped with a single reed in the mouthpiece. What might clinch the argument is that the buinnire were seated at the King's feasts at Tara alongside the players of the corn (trumpet).

The modern tinwhistle belongs to the species of musical instruments called flageolets, of which the recorder is a familiar example. The terms "whistle flutes" or "fipple flutes" are also used to designate flageolets and refer to the method of sound production. The fipple is an apparatus formed by a small plug or block, usually of wood, set into the mouthpiece, or, in some cases, is part of the mouthpiece itself. The fipples in the bone flutes from the Middle Ages were made of clay. A small space or duct is created between the edge of the fipple and the inside wall of the instrument; the player's airstream is directed by this fipple/duct system against a sharp edge or lip that is cut into the tube below the fipple, thereby producing sound. This type of vertically-blown flute became known to Europe around the 11th century, according to musicologists, and exists today in various forms throughout the world.

These tinwhistles were available in the 1902 Sears and Roebuck catalogue.

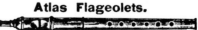

Flageolets enjoyed their peak of popularity in Europe during the Renaissance and Baroque epochs and had a revival in France and England during the late 18th and early 19th centuries. It was at this time that a great deal of experimentation was introduced in materials, design, and key and fingering systems. Though occasionally used in 18th-century orchestra works to fill the role now played by the piccolo (and also during the mid-1700s used to train singing birds), the flageolet has always been a favorite of amateur musicians.

There is no reason to believe that some form of the flageolet was not also popular in Ireland during this period. Wind instrument makers flourished in the major Irish cities from 1750-1850. Andrew Ellard, "a maker of Flageolets, Double and Triple Flutes", kept a shop at 27 Lower Sackville Street from 1819-1822 and at 47 Lower Sackville Street from 1822-1838. Joseph and James Corbett of 39 Patrick Street in Limerick also advertised flageolets from 1801-1814. Exactly when the tinwhistle now used in Irish music assumed its present form cannot be precisely determined due to the lack of contemporary documentation. By 1800 English flageolet-makers were using an adaptation of recorder fingering, and, in a sense, the modern tinwhistle can be considered a simplified version of the recorder. References to the flageolet or tinwhistle in 19th-century sources invariably describe it as an instrument that served as a means of initiating the prospective flute player or uileann piper into the idiom of Irish music, and, to a large extent, that is the role it generally played until comparatively recently. In keeping with the shady public image held by cuisleannach in medieval Ireland, it might be noted that in French, "flageoleur" denoted "a piper, a whistler, a cheater, a notable deceiver". Perhaps the next phase of research in this area should focus on what these musicians did to deserve such unflattering reputations.

There were few solo performances by tinwhistle players on commercial 78 rpm recordings made in the first half of the 20th century: Eddie Meehan, Tinwhistle O'Malley, Dan Moroney played the instrument on a few tracks. Only within the last few years has the potential of the tinwhistle as a solo instrument in its own right begun to be realized. Seán Ó Riada's innovative ensemble conceptions of Irish music gave the tinwhistle room to move and be heard on its own. Groups like the Chieftains, De Danann, Bothy Band, Planxty, and others have shown how the tinwhistle can play in twos and threes with harmonies and counterpoint. There are now also players who concentrate solely on the tinwhistle and could be said to have helped bring a standard of virtuosity to the instrument that it has heretofore lacked: Mary Bergin, Seán Potts, and Donncha Ó Brían are three names that spring immediately to mind. This tinwhistle tutor has been written in the belief that the present standard of excellence must not only be maintained but extended.

CHOOSING A TINWHISTLE

There are several types of tinwhistles commonly used by Irish musicians. The oldest is the Clarke brand that consists of a single thin metal sheet folded over on top of itself to form the joint. It is conically-tapered with the wide end at the top; the body is mostly circular except at the top where it assumes a rectangular shape with rounded corners and dimensions of approximately 5/8" by 3/4". A small block of wood is set into the top to form the fipple; a space of about 1/8" between the top of the wood and the inner metal wall serves as the duct directing the player's breath against the lip that is cut into the tube about 5/8" from the top end. The Clarke is pitched a whole tone below concert pitch, with the bottom note giving middle C. I have been told that at one time the Clarke was manufactured in D, and, if this is true, one wonders why it is not produced in concert pitch today, as it is the practice of playing in concert pitch (or sometimes higher) that has reduced the currency of the Clarke C whistle among Irish musicians. Its soft, breathy, flute-like tone is also a liability when playing with other instruments in a session. Still, for solo playing in a setting where volume and sharpness of attack are not of burning importance, the Clarke can be a very satisfying tinwhistle to play and to listen to.

The Sweetheart Flute Company of Enfield, Connecticut has taken the Clarke idea one step further and produced tinwhistles that are similar in shape to the Clarke (conical, plastic block in the head) but pitched in D. This way, the tone quality of the Clarke is preserved, and the whistle is more adaptable for general use.

The Kelischek Workshop for Historical Instruments has come up with the loudest whistle, if volume is a necessity. Made of high-grade plastic, they are cylindrical in shape with a cedar woodblock in the head. Marketed under the brand name "Susato", they are reminiscent of what flageolets were like in the 18th and 19th century; the bore is large and provides for a smooth tone throughout the range of the instrument. They are more expensive than any other kind of whistle, but they are hand-made. They also have a small thumb-rest for those who enjoy that convenience. They are pitched in D.

The Generation brand of tinwhistle comes in six sizes, designated by their bottom note—Bb (actually pitched two whole tones below concert pitch), C, D, Eb, F, and G. The D whistle is the one most favored by musicians since it is in concert pitch and can therefore be played with other concert-pitch instruments. The Generation whistles are made of cylindrical metal tubing and topped by a plastic mouthpiece that incorporates the fipple, duct, and lip. This device gives

9

the Generation a tonal brilliance lacking in the Clarke and allows for a much more distinct articulation and a clearer, cleaner sound with fewer audible overtones. The Generation also requires less wind to blow, thereby permitting the playing of longer phrases between breaths. However, I have noticed that, for some reason, the Clarke C whistles are more closely in tune with pitch standards than are the Generation key of C whistles. You will quickly discover that there are frequent variations in the pitch accuracy and sound quality of most brands, and, if you acquire a good whistle that is clear and well-tuned, hang on to it, because it might not be easy to get another one as good.

Another advantage of the Generation over the others is that the tuning is adjustable to a degree, due to the mouthpiece being a separate entity distinct from the tube. By dipping the top of the mouthpiece into a pot of boiling water, the glue anchoring the mouthpiece to the tube is usually melted, and the mouthpiece can be slid higher to conform to a lower pitch when necessary. Fiddlers occasionally tune their instruments slightly below concert pitch, and there are several bagpipes also pitched a half-tone or so low. Be careful not to leave the mouthpiece in boiling water too long, or the plastic will melt and form an interesting but unplayable piece of avantgarde plastic sculpture. And, of course, perfect tuning at the new pitch cannot be guaranteed, either, every time you move the head since the holes do not change, and internal tuning may not always be precisely on the money.

Most people buy a tinwhistle pitched in D when starting as it is concert-pitched and will permit them to play with most other instrumentalists without necessitating retuning or using alternate keys or strange fingerings. For the sake of variety, you might want to pick up some of the other keys. The F and G tinwhistles are best suited to players with extremely small hands and very thin fingers, because of the short distance between fingerholes. They are also quite shrill in the upper octave. C and Eb are most often played besides the D, though the big Bb is sometimes heard on records now and again. I have seen homemade whistles that are in A or in D an octave lower than concert-pitch D. There really is no limit to what can be done with a tinwhistle when experimentation begins in earnest.

Generation whistles are covered with nickel and brass "plating", which after a fair amount of playing tarnishes, discolors, and erodes. This distresses some people but has no discernible effect on the sound or performing capacity of the instrument. For some reason, the nickel-plated Generations are more expensive than their brass counterparts. I have never detected any significant difference between the two, though a Generation company executive could undoubtedly prove enlightening in this regard. You might eventually develop a preference for one or the other, but don't feel you have been saddled with an inferior instrument if your tinwhistle source has only brass-plated whistles in stock. New tinwhistles appear all the time, turned out by enterprising makers on a small scale. The ones we've discussed here are available commercially on a large scale, but don't let me stop you from trying out any whistle that comes into your hands, or even from making your own.

HOLDING THE TINWHISTLE

The tinwhistle can be held a variety of ways; find whichever is most comfortable for you and stick with it. Right-handed people generally cover the top three holes with the index, middle, and ring finger of the left hand and cover the bottom three holes with the index, middle, and ring fingers of the right hand. Thumbs and little fingers are not used to cover holes, unless the player has an unusual hand configuration that requires a bit of improvisation. There is a Scottish whistle player who has the tops of all his fingers missing on one hand, yet his recordings indicate that he has been able to adjust quite well to the tinwhistle. Left-handed people use the same fingers but reverse hands so that the right hand covers the top three holes, and the left covers the bottom three.

Curious inconsistencies sometimes arise. Uileann piper Joe Shannon of Chicago plays the pipes and tinwhistle left-handed, depsite the fact that he does every other manual operation in his daily life as a right-handed person. What happened was that when he first picked up the whistle as a child, he used his left hand for the bottom half instead of the top; no one corrected him until he had already become too accustomed to change to the usual right-handed grip. If you are experiencing difficulty in handling the whistle comfortably, be aware of this seemingly natural tendency to use your strong hand for the bottom position.

Here's an illustration that shows my top hand slightly angled upwards so that the fifth finger is out of the way of the index finger covering the fourth hole. The bottom hand is perfectly perpendicular to the whistle.

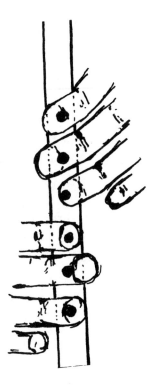

Some tinwhistle players place their fingertips directly over the holes with the fingers slightly arched, while others have the fingers extended flat with the holes covered by the part of the finger at or just before the first joint. I keep my fingers flat because it reduces the tension that results from the arched fingertip position. Tension means a loss of concentration that eventually affects my playing. The flat-fingered grip also seems to allow my fingers to move more quickly and easily in playing difficult passages and intricate embell-ishments; possibly this is on account of the greater degree of relaxation. But again, use whatever method suits your hand configuration and tension threshold.

My thumbs tend to fall naturally along the back of the whistle about parallel to where the third finger of each hand is located—the second and fifth holes—or even a bit below. The thing to remember about the thumbs is that they are the primary means of keeping the whistle balanced. Some players have the whistle in their mouth with a tight clench, but this gets fatiguing after a while, and it does your choppers a definite disservice by forcing them to chomp and grind either wood, metal, or plastic. It also makes for more tension and limits your ability to concentrate on the music, as well as making people who see your tortured and flayed whistle head think you're some kind of excessive neurotic. A death-grip with the teeth is not necessary if your thumbs are properly adjusted. You can use either or both of the little fingers to achieve a better balance. I tend to keep the little finger of my bottom hand propped against the side of the whistle a quarter inch or so below the bottom hole, while the other little finger hangs out pointing toward but not touching the whistle. Positioning the bottom hand fifth finger in this manner has the effect of easing tension rather than actually supporting the whistle. I have noticed many other players who keep both little fingers away from the instrument at all times, and they appear to be managing quite well. In this instance, as in others, the primary consideration is to eliminate tension and increase the elasticity and mobility of your fingers.

One more thing. For those of you who prefer the sound of a Clarke-type tinwhistle but suffer sore thumbs from pressing too hard against the raised seam along the back, you can fit yourself a pair of thumb-guards by cutting two small squares of thick adhesive tape and attaching them to the back of the whistle where your thumbs most generally fall. The alternative: wait it out until you develop calluses, wear gloves while playing, or switch to another make of whistle.

EMBOUCHURE

Try to blow a good strong stream of air into the whistle at all times. Blowing too hard causes squeaks and wrong notes, as you will quickly discern; at the same time, don't be too timid, or you'll never attain the clarity and sweetness of tone that makes the tinwhistle a superbly expressive instrument.

Clarke tinwhistles require more air to sound because of their mouthpiece arrangement, but Generation whistles also have their occasional idiosyncrasies. Some whistles are natural-born "lemons". and you have to adapt your airstream to cope with a whistle that is inclined to be too muffled, or, conversely, is prone to squawk under normal stress. With a Generation-type whistle, check to see that the interior opening of the fipple is evenly straight all the way across from one side to the other, as in the illustration; if it is partially closed or malformed in some way, you'll have trouble getting a clear tone.

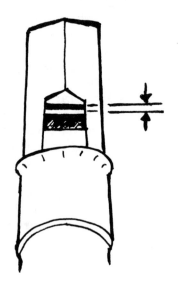

To get started, try a simple exercise that is useful for obtaining the high octave. Cover the top five holes with your fingers and blow softly into the mouthpiece. Hold it and then—without moving your fingers—blow slightly harder, tightening your lips a small amount until you've sounded the same note an octave higher. Do it until the high notes come smoothly. For variety's sake you could lift up the bottom finger and use the top four holes until all holes are open.

What just happened is that your lips shrank the size of the opening through which the air from your mouth was directed through the mouthpiece windway against the edge of the lip. You don't have to be a physics expert to realize that this forces the air out faster and in a more concentrated stream, causing the pitch to rise accordingly. Keep practicing this exercise until you get both the low and high octaves to sound smooth. After awhile it should come easily without even having to think about the technical necessities of adjusting lip pressure or air supply. And don't be afraid to really blow to reach the high notes; you'll learn fast enough how much air is needed, so don't short yourself.

Other than that, there isn't much in the way of practicing that you can do to develop your embouchure. The most relaxed way to hold the whistle in your mouth is to have the inside of your mouth touching the mouthpiece. DON'T curl your lips so that the outside part touches, as this will only bring about unnecessary strain and an absurd-looking pout. "Whistle-lips" is what the medical profession terms it.

One other method of obtaining a satisfactory tone should be mentioned, namely, the practice of pouring liquid through the tinwhistle—lubricating it, so to speak. Harmonica players occasionally soak their reeds in water before performing to loosen them up and get an easier response, and players of tinwhistles and wooden flutes in Ireland are fond of sloshing Guinness or some other beverage around the insides of their instruments. Indeed, the tone and volume of a wooden flute is temporarily improved by this expedient, but the excessive amount of moisture is damaging to the instrument in the long run and causes swelling and cracking of the wood. Wetting the wooden fipple of a Clarke tinwhistle does strengthen the tone a bit, and there isn't much that can really be ruined. However, if you have to be always running to a faucet or a water fountain before you can play, it might be simpler just to get another whistle.

FINGERING

The fingerings below are those most commonly used in playing Irish music. The fingering for the second octave is the same as for the first; notes in the second octave are obtained by blowing harder and tightening the lips, as was discussed in the previous section on embouchure.

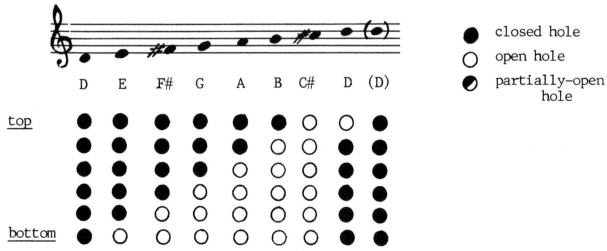

Notice that the second octave D can be played with the same fingering as the bottom D. That is, with all six holes covered, since when you're playing rapidly the difference in intonation or extra overtones caused by the top finger over the hole isn't that noticeable. Just blow harder to get the octave, and there usually isn't anything to worry about. Of course, you might find that the best intonation occurs when you use the first fingering with the top finger off; you'll certainly want to use this in airs or slow tunes or wherever the D is emphasized. The difference between the two fingerings is very noticeable when playing the flute, so if you have future plans for that instrument, it might be a good idea to get used to the slightly more awkward fingering that keeps the top hole open. Then again, you might not give a shiver for any of it.

The scale on the preceding page is for the tinwhistle in the key of D, but the fingerings remain the same for any tinwhistle; only the pitch of the notes will differ. Thus, when playing a C whistle, the note obtained when all holes are covered will be C, and uncovering the holes from the bottom one finger at a time will give a major scale of C, instead of D. You can pick up a tinwhistle in any key and play a tune using the same fingering you usually use for playing the tune; the sounds you produce will, of course, be different, but, if you're playing alone it really doesn't matter, does it? Real confusion only occurs when you try to play with someone whose instrument is pitched differently from yours.

Irish music does not generally make use of many chromatic notes. You will not have to play any accidentals other than F# or C# very often, and these just happen to be in the key of D major, as shown previously. Below are some other possibilities you will encounter, though rarely except for C-natural. Essentially, a full chromatic scale can be obtained on a whistle by partially covering the hole. Chromatic notes are "in between" the main notes of an eight-note octave scale, and this is easily observed on a tinwhistle.

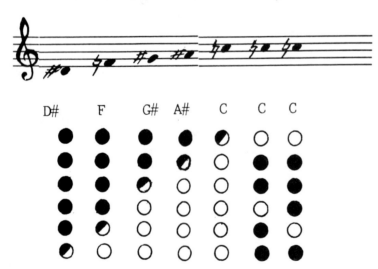

One way to obtain a "half-note" is to slide your fingertip back from the hole until you have uncovered just the necessary portion for the note you want. This is, of course, if you are moving to the chromatic pitch from the note immediately below it, say from D to D#, E to F, G to G#, A to A#, B to C-natural. Moving from a note to the chromatic note below would entail the opposite motion.

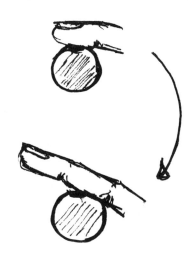

This illustration shows the motion for making the slide into a chromatic note. At the top is the finger in normal position covering a hole; at bottom, you can see how the finger has risen. The exact angle will always differ for each person and for each tinwhistle, but this is the basic technique, anyway. If you are coming to a chromatic note from a note not adjacent to it, you don't have the advantage of your finger already being in position; you can, however, slide your finger across the hole, lifting it as it moves across so that when it is in its normal position over the hole, it is also angled for the chromatic note to the proper degree. This really is more difficult to explain than to observe and do; you'll certainly have no trouble picking up on it.

With a key of D tinwhistle you can get two major keys and their relative minors without any trouble at all. The pitches in the keys of D major and B minor, G major and E minor are "built in", as it were, and the other scales in which most Irish music is located—A minor with a sharp 6th, A major with a flat 7th, D minor with a sharp 3rd, E minor with a sharp 6th, and G major with a sharp 4th are also found within the compass of normal fingerings. (In modal terms those would be A dorian, A mixolydian, D mixolydian, E dorian, and G lydian.) Partially covering holes to get notes outside this range is a bit awkward, but by assiduous practice you can greatly increase the accuracy of your intonation. It was this awkwardness and imprecision that led flute-makers to develop a complete chromatic key system for that instrument in the 19th century, and several flageolets from the early 19th century were also equipped with keys. However, until someone in a contemporary vein comes out with a fully-keyed tinwhistle (experimental models do occasionally appear), half-holing is the best you can do.

Notice that there are three fingerings given for C-natural. C-natural is a peculiar note on the tinwhistle and varies frequently in respect to its intonation depending upon the particular tinwhistle, fingering, and embouchure. Three fingerings are presented here, and there are others that sometimes produce the desired pitch; your own ear will have to be the final arbiter. The first fingering is obtained by covering a portion of the top hole. This is used for airs and in situations where you want to slide into the note. It is fairly difficult to finger accurately in playing fast dance tunes, and the second and third fingerings are recommended for that. Both the second and third fingerings are used when you want to execute an embellishment called a roll. There is some confusion on this point; some people will tell you that a roll cannot be done on C-natural, but they are referring most likely to the first fingering and are marginally correct as far as that one method of getting C-natural is concerned. However, a roll on C-natural can easily be performed by using either the second or third fingering (see the section on ornaments). Rolls on C-natural occur in numerous tunes and are an essential element of the music. I prefer the second fingering, but both are equally viable. Wendy Morrison of Washington, D.C. uses a different fingering and roll pattern for C-natural altogether, and it is not unlikely that many others do and can also.

It is crucial to gain absolute control over the basic diatonic notes, and players of the tinwhistle are really fortunate in that fingering isn't too difficult. There are many moves that are challenging, however; it's sometimes like being on a see-saw with the balance shifting continually from one end of the whistle to the other. Practice by starting at the bottom note of your whistle and work your way up through the first octave and into the second. It is useful to keep going up and down the instrument in this manner until you feel you've achieved the facility of sounding any note you want at any time. There is no need to indulge in elaborate exercises; after you have mastered the fingerings, know what the notes are in relation to each other, and can switch between both octaves with ease, you might as well start learning a tune. If you do come to a difficult passage, keep going over it. Especially troublesome for beginners is having to go from notes below the second octave D to D, up to second-octave notes, then back to D again—doing ADD EDD in a double jig, for instance. Or in a reel doing a maneuver like E in the low octave up to notes like B and second-octave D—listen to the tune "Drowsy Maggie" and you'll understand, or "The Pigeon on the Gate" or "Toss the Feathers". Once you get playing tunes, you'll find out quick enough what we're talking about here. Just make sure your fingers are relaxed and covering the holes completely, and the rest will come naturally.

ARTICULATION

While articulation is an important aspect of good tinwhistle playing, it is perhaps the most difficult concept to reduce to a pattern or formula. Articulation relates to the manner in which a note is "attacked" or enunciated; by articulating a note in a certain way, emphasis and accent are added, and the music is separated into distinct units, or phrases. The knowledge and use of articulation techniques is the key to proper phrasing, and phrasing is one of the chief means of highlighting the nuances and subtleties that give life, color, and meaning to Irish music. Listen to some of the tinwhistle players listed in the discography; each one has a distinctive approach towards articulating a tune.

The tongue, the mouth, and the fingers are the articulating agents used in tinwhistle playing. Different styles use different means of articulation, with some placing more importance on the tongue, while others make more use of the fingers and rarely use the tongue or mouth. It should be noted here that it is a good idea to listen to how other instrumentalists articulate Irish music. Style in Irish music is a very fluid thing, and cross-influences between the different instrumental traditions have produced some interesting stylistic traits. Obviously, you'll be able to discern the connection between the tinwhistle and the flute and uileann pipes, but listening to the way a fiddler digs into a note or how a concertina player phrases a passage can be very illuminating as well.

Pick up the tinwhistle, play a note, and hold it for several seconds. Move your tongue to the front of your mouth to where it touches the mouthpiece and covers the hole where the air enters. Keep blowing while you do this. Move the tongue away from the mouthpiece and then quickly touch it to the mouthpiece again. Do this several times, all the while keeping a steady airstream coming from the throat. Moving your tongue to the front of the mouth and closing the mouthpiece slit interrupts the flow of air. When this phenomenon is controlled and introduced at certain moments during the course of a tune, it is a very effective means of articulation known as "tonguing".

Practice this basic pattern of blowing a note and stopping it from sounding with the tongue until it can be done quickly and comfortably. Then try starting a note by releasing the tongue from the mouthpiece at the same time you begin to blow into the whistle. Practice this a few times and then go up and down the scale of the tinwhistle, tonguing each note as you go; lightly tapping the mouthpiece with the tongue as if pronouncing the letter "T" as in the word "tub" will achieve the necessary results.

After you can go up and down the scale tonguing each note clearly, you can try tonguing the same note in a triplet configuartion, as in the examples below.

1   2   3a   3b

4a   4b

To articulate examples 1 and 2, the action of the tongue is notated syllabically as T-T-T, with each T representing a tap of the tongue against the mouthpiece. In tonguing rapidly-played staccato triplets of this kind, a technique known as double-tonguing is sometimes resorted to, particularly in the case of examples 3a and 3b where the note following the triplet is the same pitch as the notes immediately before it and, therefore, must also be tongued to maintain clarity. In this instance the usual method can be used, but this is often awkward and hard to perform smoothly. With double-tonguing, however, the second note of the triplet receives less emphasis than the others and is articulated in an indirect manner. Syllabically, this pattern is notated as T-L-T-T. The L is a "dark" L as in "bottle", and it indicates that the tongue is raised slightly and withdrawn from the front of the mouth to touch the palate just behind the teeth and quickly lowered and brought to the front again to strike the mouthpiece with the T articulation. The action of the tongue blade (not the tip) in touching the roof of the mouth is what actually breaks the airstream between the first and second notes. Double-tonguing of this kind is not often called for in Irish music, but it occasionally comes in handy. Examples 4a and 4b show a possible use of double-tonguing to execute a quadruplet figure in both a reel and a jig.

Varying the shape of the mouth by relaxing and tensing the muscles of the lips, jaw, and cheeks also produces certain variations in articulation. I've never heard tinwhistle players discuss this; it seems to occur instinctively, and there are no set rules for applying it. Play a note without any articulation at all; then tense your facial muscles as if you were smiling. You should be able to hear a slight difference in the sound of the note. Now play a series of notes. Play them first without any articulation, then smile as you play the first note and relax the muscles again quickly as you play the second and remaining notes. Again, there is a noticeable difference. When combined simultaneously with a stroke of the tongue, a single or double grace note, and a slight bit of extra force in the airstream, the result is an added punch to the articulation of the first note. While this may seem trivial, it is a device tinwhistle players often use to introduce some spirit and lift into their playing.

Vibrato is also used by wind players to vary the tone and resonance of a note. As the term implies, vibrato is a slight wavering or vibrating of a pitch so that the intonation rises and falls smoothly and evenly. It is not common in the playing of dance tunes (though sometimes used by fiddlers who don't do embellishments) but can create a nice effect in airs, where it generally adorns the end of a phrase or a note held for a long time at a peak point in the tune. It can be played slow or fast, depending on the effect one wishes to convey. Vibrating the lips to produce fluctuations in the pitch is one method; creating pulsations in the flow of the airstream as it leaves the throat and enters the mouth is another. The syllables ooh-ooh-ooh are often used to articulate these pulsations; the tongue is often not used at all. The most common technique among tinwhistle players is to shake the finger that is two or more holes below the note being vibrated. Play a G in the low octave and began trilling the fifth finger over the E hole. Add the sixth finger over the D hole, and the vibrato will increase slightly. Play an A and shake the fourth finger over the F# hole while maintaining the A. Add the fifth finger and then the sixth to the trill, and the vibrato will vary. Using two or more fingers for the vibrating can reduce the clarity of the vibrato unless they open and close their respective holes at precisely the same moment. This is especially noticeable in the high octave.

If you have formerly played orchestral music, you will undoubtedly be familiar with vibrato, but it is important to control the natural tendency to use it too often. Its occurrence in Irish music is generally implied rather than broadly stated; subtlety is the watchword here.

A more commonly used expressive device is the slurring of notes by sliding into them from a pitch a tone or less below. This form of articulation puts the "nyea" into the music by producing a "lonesome" sound. Slurring, like vibrato, should not be overused. It is very effective in airs but can also add expression to dance tunes by introducing a brief instance of syncopation that alters the rhythmic flow and injects an element of surprise and spontaneity into the tune. You slide into a note the same way as you start to make a half-note (see the section on fingering). Slurring is a good way to really emphasize a phrase or an embellishment.

Tinwhistle styles are often characterized as being either predominantly staccato or legato. These terms refer to the relative frequency of articulation, with a staccato style using a great deal of articulation and a legato style using it less often and less obviously. Staccato favors tonguing, while legato concentrates on articulation through fingering. Staccato playing also produces short phrases that are often spit out in a vigorous, strongly-accented, somewhat aggressive manner, while legato playing seeks to minimize the effect of breaks in the melody by using long phrases in which legato triplets and rolls maintain an impression of fluidity and evenness. For a good contrast listen to the way the tune "The Green Groves of Erin" is played by Miko Russell on Traditional Country

Music of County Clare and by P.J. Crotty on Le Chéile's Lord Mayo LP. They're playing the same tune, but what a difference in articulation! The middle ground between these two extremes is perhaps the ideal direction for you to orient your playing in the initial stages. You will discover for yourself that some tunes sound their best when rendered in a legato manner, while others are greatly enhanced by considerable use of the tongue to emphasize the rhythm and to delineate phrases. Again, there is no blueprint for reproducing a style of articulation; listening to other players (especially other instrumentalists) is the only certain way to obtain full comprehension of this aspect of tinwhistle playing.

ORNAMENTS

Ornaments are used to decorate or embellish the melody. Irish music is essentially monophonic, or single-line, and the use of ornaments helps to sustain interest by presenting the melodic line in a slightly different manner each time. Ornaments also serve to fill in sections of the melody and can be used to articulate notes and shape phrases. Though some musicians make little use of ornaments, proper ornamentation can greatly enhance a tune by contributing variety, fluidity, excitement, and expressiveness.

One occasionally hears dire warnings against the dangers of what adjudicators at Irish music competitions are fond of calling "over-ornamentation"; the term is flaunted in a fashion similar to phrases such as "Red Menace", "Yellow Peril", "Yankee Imperialism", and so on. Generally, those who levy such accusations are unable to perform much ornamentation either because of an ignorance of what to do or an inability to do it.

Critics of "over-ornamentation" have missed the point altogether, for it is not the number of ornaments one uses or their density per tune or measure that is really the target of criticism. The problem is, in fact, one of misplaced ornaments—ornaments being inserted at inappropriate points of a tune so that the phrasing is obscured rather than highlighted by the ornamentation. While it is true that some players use a great deal of ornamentation in comparison to others, there is absolutely nothing wrong with doing so. The problem is not of quantity but quality. The number of ornaments is irrelevant; rather, it is the contexts in which they are used in relation to the overall performance of the tune that should be the paramount consideration governing their use. It's like using adjectives in your speech; the more you use the more colorful, evocative, and expressive your speech becomes. But, obviously, if your adjectives obscure your general meaning in the sentence, they're of little value. So don't be bullied by critics of the dreaded "over-ornamentation"; mostly it's a case of the fox looking up at those delicious grapes just out of his reach and deciding that they're probably sour anyway.

The tinwhistle is especially well-suited for playing ornaments, and every type of ornament used in Irish music is possible on the tinwhistle. Ornaments are also much easier to execute on the whistle than on other instruments, and there is really no reason not to attempt them. Each individual will make his or her own decision concerning the usage of ornaments, but it can be stated with certainty that a full knowledge of ornamentation techniques is crucial for bringing the best out of the tinwhistle.

Ornaments used in Irish music include grace notes, triplets, rolls, crans, and trills. Within each of those categories are various subtypes of ornaments. For the sake of completeness, the entire spectrum of ornaments has been discussed here; however, the reader should not feel compelled to use every one simply because they exist.

There are single, double, and triple grace notes, with the single and double

variety being the most common.
of the note it graces, yet it
rhythm of the tune. Grace
and are played very quickly.
what the name suggests; some
single grace note can be used
pitch that occur successively
tongue could also be used in
articulation, but sometimes a
desirable. The other examples
"kick off" a note group with a
attack.

A grace note shortens the duration
is not counted in with the regular
notes exist "in-between" the beats
The single grace note is exactly
examples are given below. The
to separate notes of the same
as in examples 1,2,6,7,8,12; the
these cases to achieve distinct
single grace note is more
show single grace notes used to
bit of additional momentum and

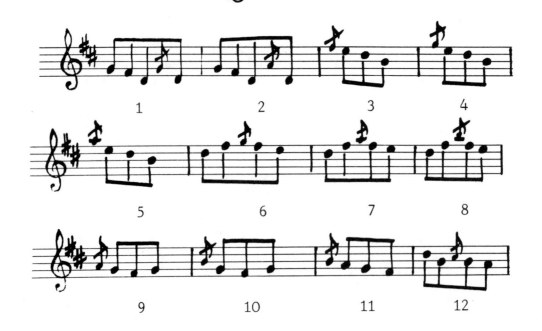

In examples 6,7,8, an F# is graced by G, A, and B. G is the most common gracing for an F#, but the other two can also be used. Example 6 is achieved by lifting the G finger (3rd finger, top hand) and setting it down again very rapidly before playing the F#. The F# finger (fourth finger) is maintained on the hole while the grace note is played; the quick opening and closing of the G hole provides just enough venting to up the pitch above the F#. If the A finger is used, the same pattern asserts itself except that the second finger is lifted and closed while the others are kept down to form the normal F# fingering. Study the tablatures of the examples on the next page.

Here's how to read these tablatures: each vertical series of six circles represents a finger movement or position. Read from left to right and simply follow the fingerings from one to the next. This is the most graphic and unambiguous method I've found for showing complicated fingerings on the tinwhistle.

The grace note is always some note above the principal note being graced. Usually it is the note directly above, as in examples 6,9,11,12. For D and E, the G and A fingers are generally used for gracing, though E is sometimes more conveniently graced by F#. With all single grace notes the pattern outlined here holds true—a rapid opening and closing of the hole just prior to playing the principal note. C natural and C# are not usually graced, but by playing the second octave D and lifting off either the fifth or fourth finger to sound C natural, a single grace note for C natural can be closely approximated.

It will do no harm to gain facility in using various fingers to execute single grace notes for the same principal note. Play each of the short note groups in the examples without the grace note; then practice putting the grace note in until you've mastered it. Using the tongue to articulate the single grace note is also an effective means of accenting the principal note. Try tonguing just as your gracing finger is coming back down over the hole and notice the sharper "bite" the grace note has.

The double grace note is similar to the single grace note except that it uses the principal note itself as the basic part of the ornament in addition to the note directly above the principal note. Looking at the following examples you can see that a double grace note is, in one sense, an unequally-weighted triplet with the first two notes played much more quickly than the third member. Again, the double grace note is played in a sort of "timeless" vacuum between principal notes; the first note of the double grace note is the same pitch as the principal note and is followed by lifting and replacing the same finger used to obtain a single grace note. Study the examples and tablatures carefully and play through them. The trick to double grace notes is not in the fingering but in the timing.

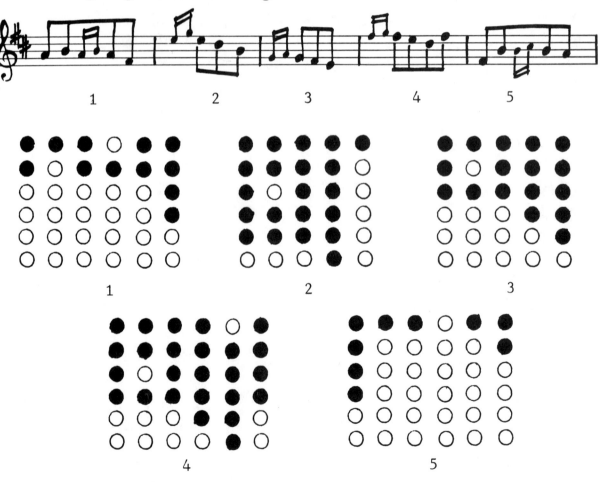

Triple grace notes may legitimately be called an extravagance. They are not something a beginner will want to get involved with; indeed, few players, beginners or otherwise, seem inclined to bother with them. They do add a sort of a flourish when used, and I would be remiss if I did not mention them. They are played by adding an extra gracing finger to the usual pattern, so that there are two fingers instead of one being lifted and replaced. Only E, F#, G, and A are generally graced in this way.

The top two fingers (A and B fingers) are used for triple gracing. To triple grace G, the B finger is lifted and dropped immediately after lifting and dropping the A finger. This is the pattern for the other notes as well, and it is easier to execute than to explain. Experimentation will undoubtedly yield other methods of introducing intricate gracing patterns in special situations. The double grace note on E can be extended to form the configuration shown in example 4 above by using both the G and F# fingers. The G finger is lifted and dropped before the F#; the A finger could also be used instead of the G.

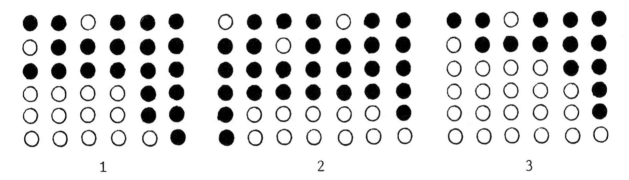

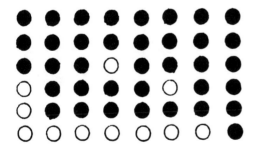

These extended gracings are not crucial to Irish music and often occur spontaneously rather than according to conscious plan. Still, it does no harm to be aware of them while taking care not to overuse or misuse these ornaments. I might also mention that some players speak of "cutting" and "tipping". "Cutting" refers to the first grace note (the cut) above the principal note; "tipping" refers to the grace note below the principal note (the tip) that occurs during an ornament called a roll to be discussed shortly. Vocabulary to describe ornaments varies among musicians. The important thing is just being able to do whatever it's called.

A triplet consists of three evenly-timed notes played in the same time as two notes are normally played. Triplets can be played in jigs where the basic note group is three eighth notes to a group (example 1); they can also be played in reels, hornpipes, and polkas that have two or four eighth notes to a note group (example 2). Part "a" of each example shows the usual pattern, while "b" indicates the form the note group takes when played as a triplet.

Triplets can be of the form found in example 3b where an extra note is tacked on to the end of each group of two notes (3a) to add a sense of fluidity and smoothness to the descent. The triplets in example 4b have been formed by inserting an extra note between the two original notes in the group and again heighten the thrust of the descening passage.

Staccato triplets are played by tonguing the note three times in rapid succession. Some tinwhistle players use a staccato triplet in place of roll when confronted with such a situation. Second octave D is often treated in this manner (examples 5 and 6) because of the difficulty in getting a consistently perfect roll. C natural is another note that is frequently played as a staccato triplet rather than as a roll (example 7), though there is less justification for this than there is with D.

There are certain passages where triplets fit well, while there are others where they disrupt the melodic and rhythmic flow. Proper use of triplets, like all embellishments, must be learned by trial and error and by listening to other players.

There are long rolls and short rolls and single and double-cut rolls. The single roll is the most basic and should be mastered before moving onto double-cut rolls. Long and short designate the duration of the roll, with a long roll spanning the time it takes to play three eighth notes and a short roll covering the time taken by two eighth notes. Anywhere there is a dotted quarter note or three eighth notes of the same pitch or three eighth notes of adjacent pitches, a long roll can replace them. A short roll can be used instead of a quarter note or two eighth notes *rolls* of the same pitch. This will become more clear when you start playing the tunes in the next section. For now it is a good idea to think of doing rolls as an alternative method of structuring a tune. Instead of playing every note in a melody as it comes along in a horizontal fashion, one eighth note after another without pause or respite, rolls help you play the tune with lots of points for emphasis. When playing with rolls, you are thinking vertically, so to speak, and your music becomes oriented toward peaks in a tune, instead of simply plodding or streaking along from start to finish. Though rolls may be difficult to master at first, in the long run you'll find that it's easier to play a tune using rolls at key points than to finger every single eighth note. It's like flying in a jet as opposed to driving a rickshaw, though there will always be some who insist on taking the more tortuous "scenic" route.

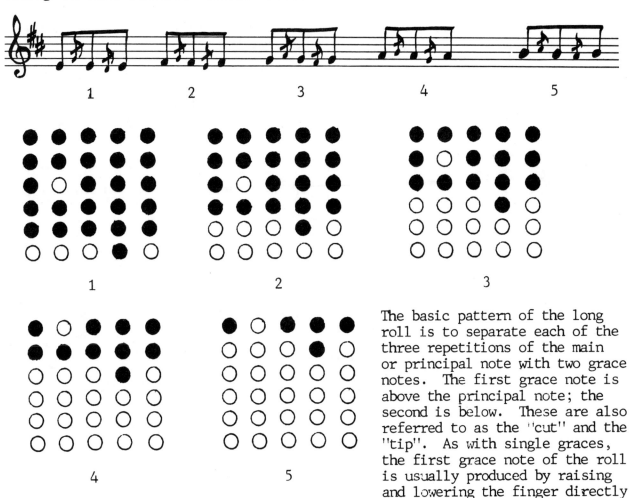

The basic pattern of the long roll is to separate each of the three repetitions of the main or principal note with two grace notes. The first grace note is above the principal note; the second is below. These are also referred to as the "cut" and the "tip". As with single graces, the first grace note of the roll is usually produced by raising and lowering the finger directly above the principal note; E is an exception in that it is graced by a G or A finger rather than F#, and F# can

also be graced by the finger two holes above it. The second grace note in a
long roll is always the note directly below the principal note. Study the
tablatures on the preceding page. Work through them slowly bearing in mind
that ultimately they must be sounded evenly. The second principal note is
actually shorter than an eighth note but has been notated as it has to give a
better idea of the theoretical concept of a roll. In practice, the long roll
assumes a variety of rhythmic forms, depending on the individual player. Rolls
on C natural, C#, and D are exceptions to the basic pattern and will be
discussed later.

Notice that in all the tablatures the principal note is like an anchor;
it never moves. When doing a B roll, the B finger has to move, of course,
but with the others, the bottom finger always remains right where it is. You
might be tempted to lift it up but should restrain this impulse. If you keep
the bottom finger over the hole throughout the roll, you'll get a crisper and
more consistently even sound.

The short roll is lacking the first statement of the principal note;
otherwise, it works the same way as a long roll. The tablatures for long rolls
apply to the short roll if you eliminate the first step and start with the
grace note above the principal note. Most beginners find short rolls hard, and
rightly so, since it's like jumping right into a roll without being able to set
yourself. The first statement of the principal note in a short roll is also
somewhat shorter than an eighth note, sounding closer to example 1b below.
Again, this will become much more clear when you begin using rolls in tunes.

Rolls on C natural, C#, and D are also possible,
though they must be accomplished by special fingerings. The tablature for a C natural long roll
appears below.

1a   1b

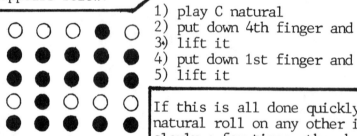

1) play C natural
2) put down 4th finger and
3) lift it
4) put down 1st finger and
5) lift it

If this is all done quickly it is the equivalent of a C
natural roll on any other instrument. Work through it
slowly a few times, then bring it up to normal speed and
witness the amazing metamorphosis of five disparate sounds
into a smooth C natural roll. If you are using the other
forked fingering for C natural, here is the tablature for
obtaining that roll. To my ear, however, the first
method gives a slightly more distinct and more
clearly defined roll. Short rolls on C natural
may be achieved by eliminating step 1.

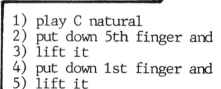

1) play C natural
2) put down 5th finger and
3) lift it
4) put down 1st finger and
5) lift it

1   2   3   4   5

The C# roll is something different altogether. Keep the bottom three fingers
on the whistle throughout the roll and simply drop your other three top fingers
over their respective holes one at a time in succession, lifting each finger

before the next one is dropped, and ending up with only the three bottom fingers still on the whistle. The top three fingers descend in a kind of bouncing motion, and the bottom three fingers act as an anchor for them. If this is done

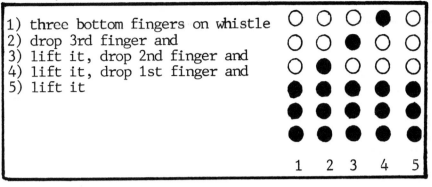

1) three bottom fingers on whistle
2) drop 3rd finger and
3) lift it, drop 2nd finger and
4) lift it, drop 1st finger and
5) lift it

slowly it is rubbish; if done at proper speed and with precise evenness, it can easily pass as a C# roll. Rolls on C# are not often encountered, but they do occasionally appear and can be made by means of this tablature.

The roll on D in both octaves is something called a <u>cran</u>. It is derived from uileann piping technique. Like the roll, the cran is essentially the principal note repeated three or four times with a grace note of some other pitch separating each repetition. With the low D, since there are no other holes below it, the grace notes are all above the D. With the high D, it is possible to use the C# below it, but this is usually not as efficient as using the same fingering used for the cran in the octave below.

A cran can really be done on nearly any note, and there are a number of forms it may take. Most crans include three or four graces, but it is conceivable that more could be introduced if desired. The crans shown here have been adapted to suit the tinwhistle and can be used in the same situations as a roll.

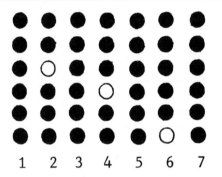

1) all fingers down for low D
2) lift 3rd finger and
3) drop it giving D again
4) lift 4th finger and
5) drop it giving D again
6) lift 6th finger and
7) drop it giving D again

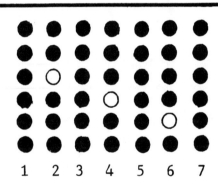

1) all fingers down for low D
2) lift 3rd finger and
3) drop it giving D again
4) lift 4th finger and
5) drop it giving D again
6) lift 5th finger and
7) drop it giving D again

What happens during a cran is that the D fingering is maintained except for very brief moments when one finger is lifted off to grace it. The tablatures above would appear in written notation as examples 1 and 2 on the next page. You can vary the basic pattern of a cran by lifting off different fingers in

1   2

different order; the base of D is always retained, however. For instance, you could lift off fingers 2,4,5 or 2,4,6. If you wanted to insert four grace notes you could use fingers 3,4,5,6 for gracing. Whatever pattern you choose will depend on your abilities as well as your aesthetic inclinations as to which cran sounds most appropriate to your ear.

Cranning the high D is also possible, though this has a tendency to sound fuzzy and unclear at times. The same gracing pattern can be used for the high D as was used for the low; you may find that keeping all the holes closed for the high D instead of opening the top hole will yield a cleaner tone. In some situations you might prefer to tongue out a staccato triplet rather than use a cran. For examples of crans-in-action listen to records by Willie Clancy, Pat Mitchell, Matt Molloy, Paddy Moloney, Liam O'Flynn and other uileann pipers and advanced flautists.

Double-cut rolls are often used by pipers, and I learned the technique from Chicago piper Joe Shannon who first heard it on 78 rpm records of Patsy Tuohey. Again, they are not essential, but they add a bit of color and excitement when used in an appropriate context. They are called "double-cut" because the principal note is "cut" twice by two upper grace notes before being "tipped" with a single lower grace note. The examples below give an idea of the basic form of this roll.

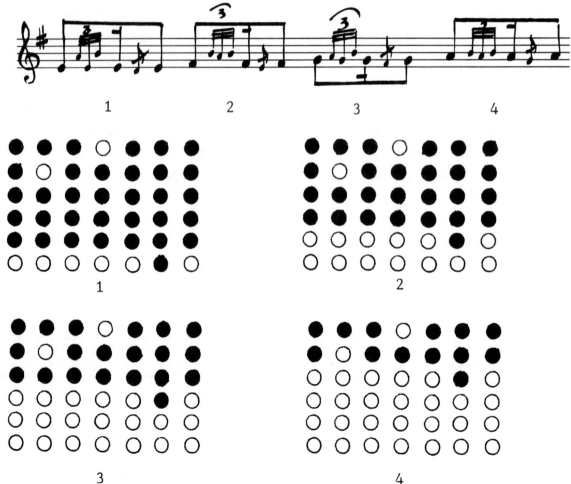

E, F#, G, and A can take a double-cut roll. As with the triple grace note, the top two fingers are used. You can try putting a double-cut roll where you would normally use an ordinary long or short roll, especially at the end of a phrase. Short double-cut rolls can be accomplished by dispensing with the first statement of the principal note.

trills

Trills are not commonly used by tinwhistle players, as rolls have assumed the function trills might be expected to play. They are most frequently heard from fiddlers, but pipers occasionally introduce them as a special variation. Trills are also used in airs as a substitute for or an intensification of vibrato. If you wish to trill an F#, you start with the F# and rapidly alternate it with the G above, as in example 1 below. This can be done simply by moving the F# finger up and down for the duration of the trill. Example 1 is the type of trill that is found in a reel like "The Bucks of Oranmore", while example 2 is taken from the third-to-last bar of "Sí Bheag, Sí Mhór". There's not much else to them, really.

1   2

This description of ornaments does not exhaust the possibilities in this area of tinwhistle playing but enumerates those patterns that have become standardized over the years. As your facility with the instrument increases, you might very likely discover new variations on these methods. If you can execute the ornaments listed here with a reasonable competence and are able to control the various articulatory devices discussed in the preceding section, then you might as well move on to the next section and start putting it all together.

29

PUTTING IT ALL TOGETHER

In this section four tunes will be presented. Each of the tunes will be given in a straight, unornamented setting that will subsequently be amplified, extended, and varied through the course of three successive versions. In this way it is hoped that the possibilities of ornamentation, articulation, phrasing, and variation can be demonstrated. Written notation has certain limits, however, and a full transcription in which each detail of performance is captured is not possible here. Also, after learning the tunes in these settings, it would be an excellent idea to find settings of the tunes from other sources and exercise the inalienable right of traditional musicians to adapt and absorb from the playing of their peers.

Four common mistakes people often make when first approaching Irish music:

1) they play the tune entirely too fast
2) they play the tune the way they think it should sound
3) they learn one version of the tune and ignore all others
4) they concentrate on only one aspect of the tune's performance and
   ignore all others

The first point should be obvious. If you play too fast you lose the rhythm, obscure the melody so that it becomes gibberish, and make it impossible for anyone to play with you. The second point emphasizes that there is no substitute when starting for learning directly and completely from appropriate models of proven value. Before you start doing your own thing with a tune, make sure you know what people have done before you. You have to hear the music live, tape it, take it home and study it very closely. Take what you've heard and learn to reproduce it exactly as it was played. Otherwise, you'll always be playing a facsimile, a pseudo-music, an almost-but-not-quite-for-real type of music that isn't rooted in the reality of the tradition. The third item brings up the necessity for constantly expanding your in-depth knowledge of a tune by learning several versions of it, or at least acquainting yourself with them. There is no One Absolute True and Perfect Setting of a tune that existed in the beginning and will last till world without end, amen. Compared to jazz, rock, classical music, or even bluegrass, Irish music uses an extremely restricted set of pitches, time units, and tone colors. Yet the creativity of Irish musicians has been stimulated by these limits, and variation in melody, rhythm, phrasing, articulation, ornamentation, and phrasing has been developed to a very sophisticated degree allowing the player to put a great deal of personal expression into the music. Learning different versions of a tune teaches you a lot about the music's structure, how different styles operate, and how you can be more creative in terms of the idiom. Point number four cautions that you've got to comprehend the tune as a whole and not get hung up on one intense aspect of the tune. The best way to sound like you know what you're doing is to do it.

A few symbols used in the transcriptions should be explained:

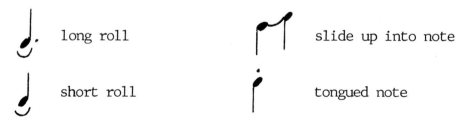

long roll

short roll

slide up into note

tongued note

When learning a tune it is best to try and grasp it as a totality by comprehending the total shape and flow, rather than picking at it in bits and pieces. Traditional players will often tell you that if you can whistle or hum the whole tune through before trying to play it, you'll be able to play it with less trouble. Or, as fiddler John Vesey once remarked, "It's not how many tunes you play but how well you play them that counts."

"Kerrigan's Jig" is the first tune to try. It was recorded in the 1920s by Sligo fiddler Michael Coleman and has had a recent reincarnation as "The Kesh Jig" by the Bothy Band. It is as good a place as any to start. Notice the tonguing suggestions, but don't let them cause any excessive confusification.

Once you can play through the tune confidently from memory, try adding some grace notes as implied in the second setting.

There are several places where legato triplets fit well. Usually the first note of the triplet is tongued to emphasize the triplet in a distinctive way within its note group.

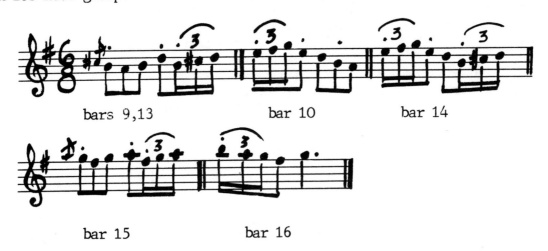

bars 9,13   bar 10   bar 14

bar 15   bar 16

Now try using rolls. Notice how rolls can completely change the cast of a tune. Phrasing, rhythm, melody—the entire character of a tune is altered.

Finally, play this setting that combines grace notes, triplets, rolls, and melodic and rhythmic variations.

This next tune is a polka that was recorded by two Kerry fiddlers, Denis Murphy and Julia Clifford, on The Star above the Garter (Claddagh CC5). They included it in a medley of polkas entitled "The Ballydesmond Polkas", but the tune has appeared more recently in Breandán Breathnach's Ceol Rince na hÉireann (Dance Music of Ireland) as "Maurice Manley's Polka". It is a good simple tune for practicing the rhythmic swing inherent in Irish polkas; there is a strong emphasis on the first beat of each measure, and you may want to dwell on this note a slight bit longer than the rest.

Now try some grace notes and triplets.

This next version incorporates some rolls.

A setting with ornaments and variations. Notice the slide into the E in the sixth bar of the first part.

This next tune will be more of a challenge. "The Wicklow Hornpipe" was collected by Francis O'Neill in Chicago in the late 1800s from two sources: Kildare-born piper John Ennis and Mayo-born fiddler John McFadden. Ennis stated the tune had been known to him as a youth in Kildare, while McFadden claimed he had first heard the tune from a flute player/singer/dancer/pub-owner in Cleveland, Ohio named Michael White—originally from Tralee, Kerry. Paddy Cronin recorded it for Copley Records of Boston in the early 1950s as "Delahunty's Hornpipe", it's on Chieftains 3 (Claddagh CC10), and some musicians in Ireland call it after Joe Ryan, a fiddler from Meath. So much for history.

Hornpipes are generally played with a very strong accent on the first and third beats of a measure, though there is a certain amount of syncopation a good player will occasionally introduce to vary this rhythmic pattern. To get the feel of hornpipe rhythm, it might be wise to treat this tune as if each group of four eighth notes were written and played as:

Hornpipes are usually played slower than reels but slightly faster than jigs, though there are many exceptions. Step-dancers of the New Style require hornpipes played excrutiatingly slow to the point of turgidity to accomodate the intricacies of the dance steps. Whatever tempo you choose, try to retain the distinctive bounce in the rhythm; otherwise the difference between the hornpipe and the reel becomes blurred as it did two centuries ago when American dance musicians absorbed tunes from the Irish repertoire.

Some grace notes and triplets.

Some rolls and a cran on the bottom D in the final bar of each section.

A setting with imaginable variations.

36

This next reel is said to have been composed by John Doherty, the Donegal fiddler who died last year in his eighties and, along with his brother Michael, typified the old style of Donegal fiddling. It is a very flexible, malleable tune well able to withstand numerous twists and turns without losing its basic character. In fact, there are several variations not shown here that fit quite nicely; you'll probably figure them out after awhile.

. . .and then. . .

37

Try this. . .

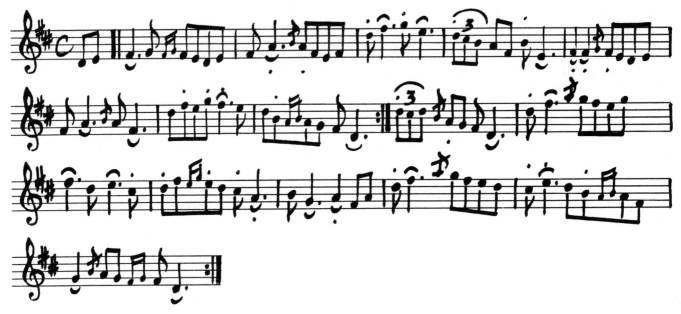

. . . .or. . .?

38

PHRASING & BREATH CONTROL

A few words should be said about the interplay of phrasing and breath control. Only rarely are rests, breathing indicators, and phrases marked in transcriptions of Irish music. It has long been the practice of editors and collectors to give all the notes of the tune, but the burden of deciding when to take a breath is placed upon the individual wind player. Practically speaking, it would be almost impossible to notate these elements in detail, especially since the possibilities for variation in phrasing and breath-taking are manifold. Pausing for breath is a necessity for players of wind instruments, but it need not be a disadvantage. If handled skillfully, breath-taking can emphatically define the boundaries between phrases while adding an element of surprise and novelty to the tune.

Any tinwhistle player possessing a healthy set of lungs can get through an eight-bar section of a tune at normal tempo without too much difficulty. There are times, however, when you don't want to interrupt the flow of a tune after each eight bars. As you've probably noticed, most Irish dance tunes consist of two eight-bar sections that can be subdivided into shorter phrase units of four and two bars each. Most tunes are also constructed so that there are points where you can take a breath and briefly break the flow of the melody without seriously violating the sense and movement of the tune or losing time or tempo. These points are often found every two bars, either just before or after the bar line between bars 2 and 3, 4 and 5, 6 and 7, 8 and the following bar of the next section. This is the general prevailing pattern, and there are exceptions that cannot be dealt with here.

Players coming from classical backgrounds often try to sneak a breath between notes in the same way that grace notes are inserted between consecutive eighth notes. Experimentation on your own will reveal that taking breaths in this way produces a halting, unstable movement, as if you tried to take a breath between syllables of a word when talking. The usual practice is to forget about playing the note that would ordinarily be played were it not replaced by a pause for breath. Instead of slipping a pause between two notes, you eliminate one of the notes entirely and use that space for your breath. This creates a gap in the melodic line and generally necessitates a rearrangement of several of the notes in the immediate vicinity of the breath-taking. This is where ingenuity in reshaping the melody and rhythm asserts itself.

Study the following examples that show how phrasing is altered when a breath is taken. The tune is "The Dunmore Lassies" and is found on Matt Molloy's solo record on Mulligan, Seamus Tansey's Best of LP on Outlet, and on various album anthologies that feature the tune in a medley of three reels by a great flute player of the pre-World War II era, Tom Morrison.* You might find a comparison of those three versions enlightening, but for the present, here are three possible methods of varying the phrasing in the second part of the tune. Example 1 shows the tune without pauses; the other examples signify a breath where an eighth-note rest appears. Play through them, and the effect of variations in breath placement will become clear.

*Try Irish Dance Music (Folkways FW8821) for the Morrison medley.

example 1

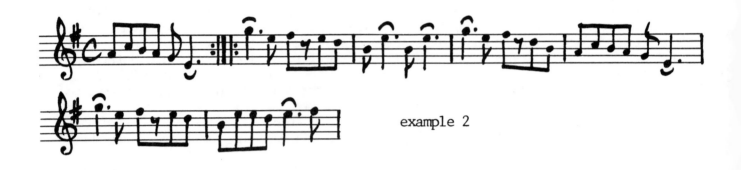

example 2

example 3

example 4

AIRS

The difficulty of notating airs has already been discussed. Some editors of Irish music collections avoid the problem by omitting airs from their works and concentrating solely on the dance music. Yet, airs are a very good introduction to Irish music, and there are eight of them included in the tunes following. The airs selected are regular and simple in structure. They are used and reused for songs in Irish and English, and their titles vary accordingly.

What really makes airs difficult to notate accurately is that they are adapted to fit the peculiarities of each verse in a song. Slight alterations in rhythm, ornamentation, and even melody occur from verse to verse. As with dance tunes, variation is an important element of the performance of the air. Adjusting the tune to the text is known as "humoring"; that is, lengthening or shortening the duration of certain notes to produce variation in the regular accent pattern. The meter is never really lost, but stretched a bit so that a greater amount of freedom is achieved between the boundaries of the bar lines. When confronted with an air in 3/4 time, it is possible that it may not be played in strict waltz rhythm but is performed slower and with plenty of humoring. Many of the airs presented in this book could also be written in 6/8; if played in this meter at a quick tempo, closer observance of the regular rhythm is generally maintained. When learning an air from written notation, it is perhaps best to learn it as written and then begin the process of humoring the melody and rhythm. Try to find a version of the air as performed by a singer, as this will best demonstrate the possibilities of variation.

Embellishments are frequently used in air-playing, especially in the slower ones. Single and double graces and legato triplets provide a sense of fluidity while attempting to reproduce ornaments used by singers. Glissando and portamento passages are also a feature of Irish singing; these are scale-like runs or slides that give the effect of gliding from one note to the next. They can be used in air-playing also, especially when moving between two notes several intervals apart. Sliding into a note from a pitch slightly below it is another device used in playing airs.

Playing airs is simpler than it might seem. Hearing the air performed by a singer or musician is an essential part of the learning process, and even if you feel you play the air well after obtaining it from a printed version, your interpretation will be even more expressive if you hear it performed live.

If you have gone through the foregoing tunes and can play all the settings with ease, there is nothing to prevent you from going on to the tunes in the next section. These tunes are designed to assist in the refinement of technique while providing a varied repertoire. Remember, they aren't given in order of difficulty, so skip around until you find a tune you like. There are many ways to play these tunes, and an attempt was made to incorporate as many variations as possible while still retaining the basic character of the tune. The versions set down here are not infallible, ultimate, or even superlative, though if you're just starting, you could do much worse than to successfully master these tunes.

There should by now be no need of notating every breath, tongue tap, or finger movement. Only rolls, triplets, and a few slides have been notated. Let your imagination run amok. As for the settings, they reflect the influence of the sources from which they came. For those curious about such things, there are some dribblets of information about the tunes following the music.

Good luck!

THE TUNES

1 Seán Ryan's Reel

2 The Steeple Chase

3 The Flowers of Redhill

43

4 The Golden Keyboard

5 The Tobercurry Reel

6 Owney Davey's Reel

44

7 Phelan's Frolics

8 Love at the Endings

9 The Maiden of Maybury

10 Charlie Lennon's Reel

11 The Boys on the Hilltop

12 O'Keeffe's Pigeon on the Gate

13 Cooley's Favorite

14 McGovern's Reel

15 A Donegal Reel

16 Ed McMahon's Fancy

17 The Shoemaker's Fancy

18 O'Connell's Welcome to Dublin

19 Redican's Jig

20 The Trip to Killavil

21 The Boholla Jig #1

22 The Boholla Jig #2

23 Martin Hardiman's Jig

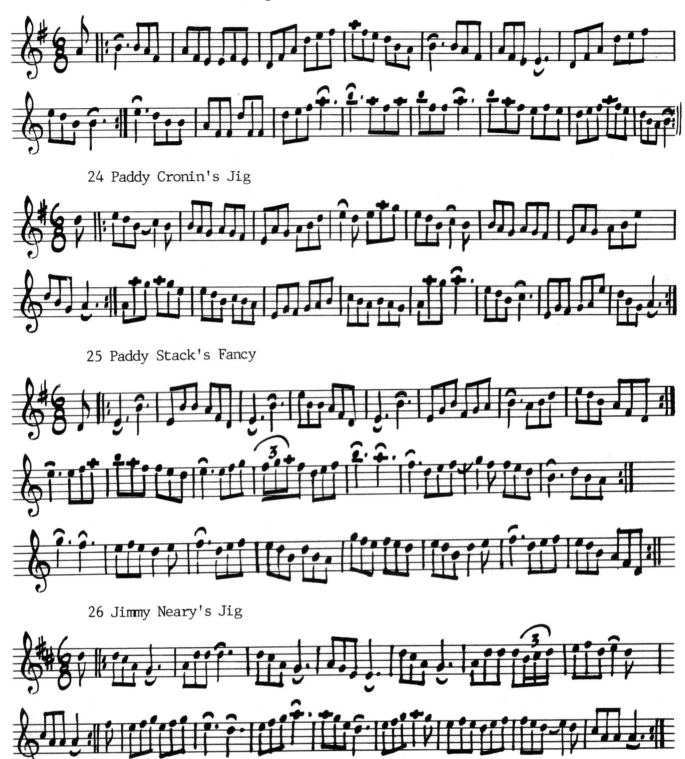

24 Paddy Cronin's Jig

25 Paddy Stack's Fancy

26 Jimmy Neary's Jig

27 The Birthday Jig

28 Higgins' Hornpipe

29 O'Callaghan's Hornpipe

30 Alexander's Hornpipe

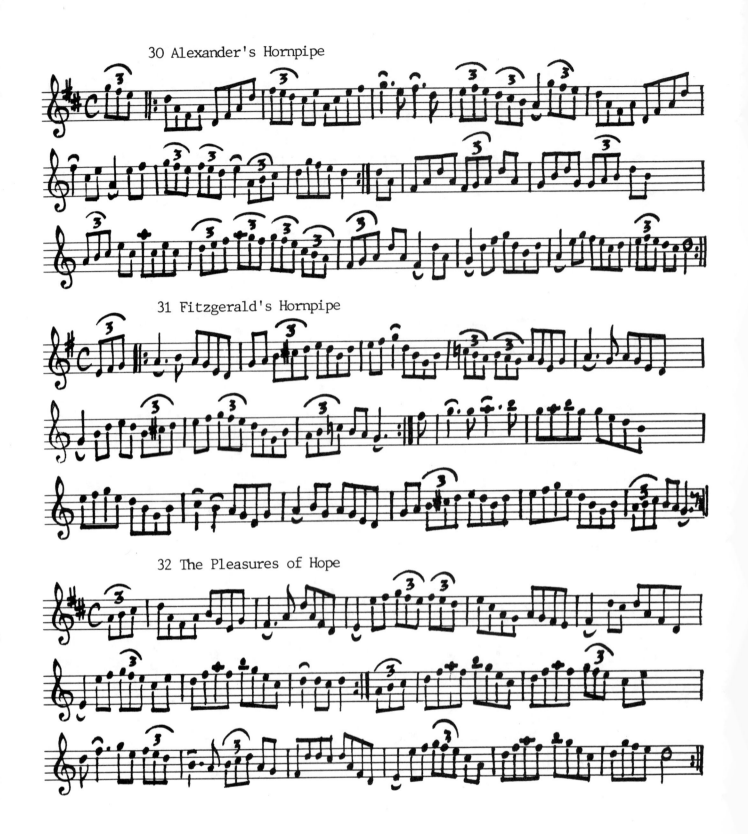

31 Fitzgerald's Hornpipe

32 The Pleasures of Hope

52

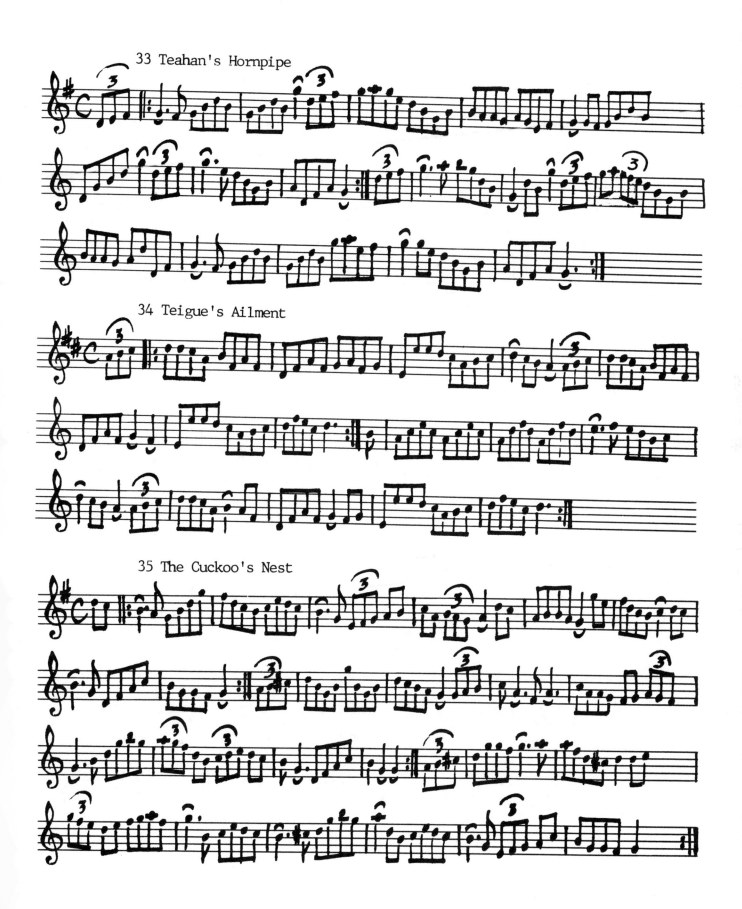

33 Teahan's Hornpipe

34 Teigue's Ailment

35 The Cuckoo's Nest

36 The Leitrim Fancy

37 The Listowel Hornpipe

38 Katie Scollard's Slide

54

39 Dust on the Bible

40 Mom's Favorite

41 My Love in the Morning

42 Tom Moran's Fancy

43 Coleman's Favorite

44 Tipperary Hills

45 Last Night's Fun

46 Give Us A Drink of Water

47 A Fig for A Kiss

48 The Queen's Polka

49 The Rainy Night under the Bridge

50 Jack Mitchell's Polka

51 Mickey Chewing Bubblegum

52 Tony Lowe's Polka

53 Tom Ash's March

54 The Irish Freedom March

55 The Blackbird

56 Rodney's Glory

57 The Job of Journeywork

58 The Reaper of Glanree

59 Sí Bheag, Sí Mhór

60 Tabhair dom do Lámh

61 Ím Bó 'gus um Bó

62 The Thatched Cabin

63 The Green Glens of Gweedore

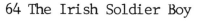

64 The Irish Soldier Boy

65 The May Morning Dew

66 Green Brooms

67 Cailín Deas Rua

68 Sullivan's John

NOTES

1. <u>Sean Ryan's Reel</u> was composed by Sean Ryan, a fiddler from Co. Laois, and was recorded on his first LP in the early 1960s for Avoca.

2. <u>The Steeple Chase</u> was recorded by the Sligo fiddler Paddy Killoran around 1930. Killoran was one of the most frequently recorded Irish musicians in the U.S. during the period between the World Wars. He owned a tavern in Manhattan for many years and died in 1965. This tune is also called <u>Ah Surely</u> and has been recently recorded by New York fiddlers Andy McGann and Paddy Reynolds on their Shanachie album.

3. <u>The Flowers of Redhill</u> is associated with the counties of Sligo and Leitrim and was recorded in the 1920s by the Leitrim flute player John McKenna. This setting derives from fiddler John McGreevy of Chicago and flute player/piper Kevin Henry of Chicago.

4. <u>The Golden Keyboard</u> was also learned from John McGreevy.

5. <u>The Tobercurry Reel</u> is also associated with Co. Sligo and was recorded in the the 1920s by fiddler James Morrison and piper Tom Ennis. Along with Killoran and Michael Coleman, Morrison's recordings were seminal in the spread of the Sligo fiddle style during the 1920s and '30s. Morrison operated an Irish music school in New York, was a ticket-taker on the subway, and died in 1947. Tom Ennis was a native of Chicago who died from a heart attack in 1931 at age 42. His style was an extension of that developed by Patsy Tuohey in the late 19th century, and had Ennis lived a few years more, American uileann piping might have taken a different course.

6. <u>Owney Davey's Reel</u> was obtained from John McGreevy who learned it from a Sligo-born flute player John met in Cleveland, Ohil named Owen Davey. It appears on the Philo album by John McGreevy and flute player Seamus Cooley.

7. <u>Phelan's Frolics</u> was composed in the early 1970s by a Dublin piper, Peter Phelan.

8. <u>Love at the Endings</u> is a composition of Ed Reavy of Philadelphia, quite likely the most prolific composer of Irish music ever. 78 of his tunes have been published in <u>Where the Shannon Rises</u> (1971). Most of Ed's tunes are best suited to the fiddle, but this reel loses nothing in the translation to the tinwhistle. For a more detailed analysis of Reavy's music, see the notes I've written for an upcoming Rounder LP of Reavy's tunes.

9. <u>The Maiden of Maybury</u> is a composition of his own the author has made bold to include. May she rest in peace.

10. <u>Charlie Lennon's Reel</u> is attributed to the Leitrim fiddler Charlie Lennon and appears on Matt Molly's solo album on Mulligan. The first part is closely related to <u>The Pigeon on the Gate</u>, but the second part is something else.

11. <u>The Boys on the Hilltop</u> was culled from a 78 recording by Paddy Killoran and Paddy Sweeney. Sweeney, like Killoran, was a native of the area of southern Sligo that spawned so many outstanding Irish musicians in the early 1900s. He died in 1974 at age 85.

12. <u>O'Keeffe's Pigeon on the Gate</u> is a unique version of <u>The Pigeon on the Gate</u> as performed by Patrick O'Keeffe, perhaps the last of the itinerant teachers of Irish music in Ireland with links to the 19th century and beyond. Though fully

qualified as a school teacher, a dispute with the authorities induced him to take up the life of a wandering minstrel. He traveled the roads of Cork and Kerry for decades until his death in 1963. Several of his pupils are still actively performing, and a brother lives in Chicago. O'Keeffe was renowned for his unusual tune settings and was also a handy composer. He may be heard on Kerry Fiddles (Topic) with two of his most famed pupils, Julia Clifford and Denis Murphy. This version of The Pigeon on the Gate was transcribed from a private tape made shortly before his death.

13. Cooley's Favorite is a reel whose origin and identity has yet to be fully ascertained. I have never heard anyone play it besides Seamus Cooley, and he forgets where he got it.

14. McGovern's Favorite was played by Sligo fiddler John Vesey, now a resident of Philadelphia, over WXPN radio in June, 1974. In his introduction to the tune, John fixed the origin of the tune as Co. Cavan, though it is clearly related to #31 in this collection. Horslips also recorded the tune a while ago on Drive the Cold Winter Away.

15. A Donegal Reel is the appellation conveniently attached to a tune I heard played by fiddlers James and John Kelly of Dublin in 1975. They had no name for it but believed they learned it during a trip to Donegal.

16. Ed McMahon's Fancy is named after a Clare musician (flute/tinwhistle/concertina) who emigrated to Pittsburgh in the early 1900s. I got the tune from Richard Hughes, a flute player, guitarist, and vocalist who was a pupil of McMahon's in the 1960s. He had no name for it, and neither of us had ever heard anyone play it.

17. The Shoemaker's Fancy is derived from Seamus Cooley's setting of an old jig.

18. O'Connell's Welcome to Dublin is the title given to this jig by Breandán Breathnach in Ceol Rince na hEireann, Vol. 2. It was recorded by fiddler Seán Ryan and flutist P.J. Maloney on their LP, Traditional Music of Ireland, Vol. 1 (Avoca).

19. Redican's Jig is attributed to Larry Redican, a Dublin fiddler who lived in New York City from 1929 until his death onstage at an Irish music concert in 1975. He was also a fine tenor banjo player, though this is not widely known. His niece, Nancy Harling, is a noted piano player in Chicago.

20. The Trip to Killavil is a common jig around the district of Killavil in southern Sligo and appeared on an album featuring musicians from that area, Music from Coleman Country (Leader).

21/22. The Boholla Jigs are part of the staple repertoire of Irish musicians in Chicago, appearing to have been disseminated by natives of Boholla, Mayo. They are often played as a medley.

23. Martin Hardiman's Jig is named for an accordion player who lived in Chicago years ago. This setting is a composite from the playing of New York fiddler Andy McGann and Chicago pianist Eleanor Neary.

24. Paddy Cronin's Jig was composed by Boston fiddler Paddy Cronin and was recorded by the author on a visit to Paddy in June, 1973. Paddy is a native of Kerry, a pupil of Patrick O'Keeffe, but well versed in other Irish fiddle styles. He plays flute and fiddle on several LPs and 78s; his brother Johnny is a noted fiddler in New York.

25. Paddy Stack's Fancy is commonly called Morrison's Jig, but this version is from a tape of Patrick O'Keeffe and has an extra part. Stack was from Kerry between Listowel and Castleisland and made a few 78s with Chicago piper Eddy Mullaney in the 1920s. A setting also appears in Francis O'Neill's Waifs and Strays of Gaelic Melody.

26. Jimmy Neary's Jig was obtained from Jimmy Neary, a Mayo-born fiddler living in Chicago since the 1920s. He and his wife Eleanor have made their home a haven for Irish musicians for decades, and this jig is but one of the may rare tunes they possess. John McGreevy recorded it on his Philo LP.

27. The Birthday Jig was composed in 1978 by a Pittsburgh plectrum player and square dance caller, Larry Edelman. He plays it on Devilish Merry's LP The Ghost of His Former Self (Wildebeest).

28. Higgins' Hornpipe was recorded by piper Tommy Reck around 1950 for Copley Records of Boston, the same company that released 78s by Paddy Cronin. Another setting is in O'Neill's Dance Music of Ireland. Flute player Noel Rice of Chicago first acquainted me with Finbar Furey's contemporary piping version of the tune.

29. O'Callaghan's Hornpipe is said to have either been composed by Patrick O'Keeffe or adapted and popularized by him. An itinerant fiddler named O'Callaghan flourished in Kerry in the generation preceding O'Keeffe, and this could be the source of the tune.

30. Alexander's Hornpipe was also recorded by Tommy Reck with Higgins', but this version is taken from piper Willie Clancy's recording of the tune on a 1950s Folkways LP that also features fiddler Michael Gorman.

31. Fitzgerald's Hornpipe was recorded by Paddy Cronin on a Copley 78 around 1950 and by fiddler Tony DeMarco on a Flying Cloud LP (Adelphi) in 1977.

32. The Pleasures of Hope is a fine hornpipe brought to my attention by accordionist/concertinist Terry Teahan of Chicago. Another setting can be found in the O'Neill collections. Terry has just published his own book of compositions, entitled The Road to Glountane, available from 5041 W. Agatite, Chicago, IL 60630.

33. Teahan's Hornpipe was recently composed by Teahan.

34. Teigue's Ailment is another unusual piece from Terry Teahan's repertoire.

35. The Cuckoo's Nest is found in printed collections as far back as 1723 and is said to have been derived from an Elizabethan English song entitled Come Ashore Jolly Tar and Your Trousers On, undoubtedly X-rated in its day. I have never heard any two musicians play the tune exactly alike, and this setting comes from several sources, perhaps originally from Willie Clancy.

36. The Leitrim Fancy is an old standard and was recorded in the 1920s by a Leitrim piper living in New York, Michael Gallagher. Gallagher made only a few commercial recordings, but those that survive show him as an accomplished exponent of the tight style of piping. The present setting has attempted to translate some of Gallagher's tight staccato triplets into a suitable whistle version.

37. The Listowel Hornpipe was recorded by New York fiddler Jackie Roche on an Avoca LP during the late 1950s. Roche was a pupil of James Morrison. This tune appears to be a hornpipe version of #53 in this collection, though which originated first, the hornpipe or the march, is impossible to determine.

38. Katie Scollard's Slide was obtained from Terry Teahan who first heard it played by a neighbor in Castleisland around 1910. Though Mrs. Scollard was then in her eighties, Terry recalls that "she was as smooth a concertina player as you'd ever want to hear."

39. Dust on the Bible is another slide from Terry Teahan.

40. Mom's Favorite is a Terry Teahan tune you won't hear every day of the week.

41. My Love in the Morning is a single jig I first heard from flute player Michael Tubridy of Clare and Dublin.

42. Tom Moran's Fancy was recorded by Westmeath accordionist John Joe Gannon on Seoda Ceoil #2 (Gael-Linn). Tom Moran was a fiddler from Gannon's home district, and John Joe states the interesting fact that the single jig, though now rarely heard, was only a generation ago as popular among musicians in that area as any other dance tune genre.

43. Coleman's Favorite is an interesting slip jig recorded by Sligo fiddler Michael Gorman who was a contemporary of Michael Coleman, perhaps the most famous of the many outstanding Sligo fiddlers of the early 20th century. Unlike most of his contemporaries, Gorman went to London instead of New York and was not "discovered" or recorded until he was late in years. This is really a simple tune that initially seems complex because of the way the phrases end on the second beat of bars 1 and 3 in the first part and in bar 2 of the second part. The slip jig danced to this tune must certainly have been something extraordinary. Gorman's version is on Irish Jigs, Reels, and Hornpipes (Folkways).

44. Tipperary Hills is the name given in O'Neill's books to the slip jig Gorman plays after Coleman's Favorite. You can also hear it on the Bothy Band's second LP.

45. Last Night's Fun is also played in E and has appeared in several 19th and 20th-century collections.

46. Give Us A Drink of Water was recorded in 1923 for Victor by piper Patsy Tuohey. Tuohey was the premiere piper in the U.S. from the 1880s until his death in 1923, and many of the tunes he recorded have become established as classics among those pipers who have followed him.

47. A Fig for A Kiss is another favorite of 19th and 20th-century Irish music editions and is known under a variety of titles and settings.

48. The Queen's Polka was obtained from Terry Teahan and fiddler/vocalist Maida Sugrue, both pupils of Patrick O'Keeffe. It appears without a name in Breathnach's Ceol Rince na hÉireann, Vol. 2 and is heard by Teahan and Sugrue on Irish Music from Chicago (Rounder), an anthology of Chicago Irish music produced by the author and Miles Krassen.

49. The Rainy Night under the Bridge is also from Terry Teahan. A different setting of the tune was recorded on The Star above the Garter (Claddagh) by Denis Murphy and Julia Clifford.

50. Jack Mitchell's Polka is the name given by Terry Teahan to a polka widely-known under a variety of aliases.

51. Mickey Chewing Bubblegum is a tune from Terry Teahan also recorded by Jackie Daly and Seamus Creagh as Bill Sullivan's Polka.

52. Tony Lowe's Polka is named for an accordion player who flourished in Chicago during the 1930s and '40s, though it probably has as many names as players.

53. Tom Ash's March is found in collections in a slightly different setting as Bonaparte Crossing the Rhine. It is also related to #37 in this book. Both the march and the one following were recorded from Frank Thornton, a Kerry flute player now living in Chicago. Tom Ash was a Kerryman who died on hunger strike while imprisoned during the Irish War for Independence in 1919.

54. The Irish Freedom March bears passing resemblance to several marches in G, but Frank Thornton's version seems unique. Both marches presented here are included on the Rounder Irish Music from Chicago record.

55. The Blackbird is believed to date back to the late 17th century in sentiment if not in actual fact. There are several dance tunes and airs that share the title along with melodic similarities, and "the blackbird" was the allegorical image used by 18th-century poets when referring to the various members of the Stuart royalty who represented the last hopes for Irish resistance in the 17th and 18th centuries. The tune is popular among musicians but seems to have lost favor with modern step dancers. This is a composite version from several sources, perhaps originally John Kelly, Sr. of Dublin.

56. Rodney's Glory commemorates a naval victory in 1782 by the British admiral Rodney over the French fleet in the West Indies. Among the seamen in Rodney's forces was one of the last of the Munster poets of the old bardic school, Owen Roe O'Sullivan, who composed a song in honor of Rodney's triumph. It is doubtful that the song was sung to the present tune, but the tune's genesis remains unclear. This version stems from a recording by Michael Gorman and Willie Clancy, and the Clancy setting is in The Dance Music of Willie Clancy by Dublin piper Pat Mitchell (Mercier Press).

57. The Job of Journeywork was recorded by Michael Coleman in the 1930s, and the setting here derives largely from that source. Coleman's music has been reissued in four albums, two by Shanachie Records and two from IRC/Intrepid Records.

58. The Reaper of Glanree is a set dance obtained from Liz Carroll (fiddle) and James Keane, Jr. (accordion) of Chicago who learned the tune from a manu-script in possession of Terry Teahan. John Doonan, a piccolo player living in England, is one source of the tune, though it seems like a recent compo-sition or a conglomeration of several tunes. There does not appear to be any set dance to it, though there are reports that the publication of this tune in the first edition of this book has stimulated at least one teacher in Washington, D.C. to create a dance for the tune.

59. Sí Bheag, Sí Mhór is believed to be the first of the Irish harper Turlough O'Carolan's 200-odd compositions. O'Carolan (1670-1738) lived during a very transitional period in Irish history, and he sought to introduce elements of the Italian Baroque style into his work for the largely Anglo-Irish nobility that patronized him. This piece was inspired by the folklore that surrounds two hills in Co. Leitrim said to be inhabited by the spirits of ancient warriors whose mortal bodies lie entombed within the hills. From time to time, these spirits revive their quarrel resulting in "great cannonading and firing of guns and bloodshed. . .to the great surprise of the country at large", according to Donal Sullivan in his O'Carolan Life and Times of an Irish Harper. This tune was put back into circulation by Seán O Ríada in the 1960s, and a 1972 recording by Planxty, featuring the piping of Liam O'Flynn, escalated its popularity immensely.

60. Tabhair dom do Lámh (Give Me Your Hand) was composed by a 17th-century Irish harper named Rory Dall O Cathain who spent much of his life in Scotland. This piece is alleged to have been composed to celebrate the peaceful resolution of a dispute between O Cathain and a patroness. As with many of the old harp tunes, it has only recently been revived. Seán O Ríada, Planxty, and others have recorded and popularized it. It was also background music for an Aer Lingus (Irish Airlines) TV commercial a few years back.

61. Im Bó 'gus um Bó is one of the oldest Irish tunes extant. It is mentioned in a 17th-century manuscript as the song to which a poet's lament for his dead spaniel is to be sung. The poet, Geoffrey O'Donoghue of Glenflesk, Kerry, died in 1670, and it is believed the tune was also used for other songs like lullabies or laments. A simple yet eloquent melody, I first heard it played by Rev. Christopher Warren of Kerry in Dublin in 1972.

62. The Thatched Cabin is a song in which the emigrant nostalgically recalls his peaceful, care-free boyhood in rural Ireland and contrasts it with his present state of unhappiness and discontent. This is the air used by Seamus Cooley in his performance of the song; there is also a setting of the tune as a reel that has been recorded by De Danann and Le Cheile.

63. The Green Glens of Gweedore is another emigrant song and the locale is the village of Gweedore in Donegal. I first heard it sung in Irish at a session in Boyle, Roscommon in 1972 by John McVeay, a fine young singer who died in August, 1975. It is also commonly the air for a song called Paddy's Green Shamrock Shore.

64. The Irish Soldier Boy is an air used for many songs and often played as a waltz at Irish dances in the U.S. The recently-composed song, A Tribute to Joe Cooley, is sung to it, and it was from Joe Cooley's sister-in-law, Mary Cooley, that I first heard the song and air.

65. The May Morning Dew is another air picked up from Mary Cooley. She can be heard performing the song on Hollow Poplar (Log Cabin), an album of the 1974 Battle Ground Old-time Fiddlers' Gathering.

66. Green Brooms relates the story of a lazy young man whose father finally forces him to go out and sell brooms; the first person who sees the young man hawking the brooms is a rich woman who marries him upon his arrival in her room, and they all live happily ever after, except for the father whose brooms remain unsold. It is one of the "classical" ballads of the British Isles, and phallic imagery is rampant. The noted sean-nós singer Seán Mac Donnchadha recorded it a few years ago for an anthology of British folksong, and I first heard Kevin Conneff of Dublin, a handy bodhrán player and singer, deliver it at a session in Slattery's.

67. An Cailín Deas Rua (The Pretty Red-haired Girl) is only one title for an air that serves as the vehicle for many songs in Irish and English.

68. Sullivan's John is a song of a traveling man, or tinker, as itinerants are often called in Ireland. I first heard the song from a Cork concertina player, Seán O'Dwyer, and it seems to have come to the world at large from a traveler and street musician named Pecker Dunne, whose version was recorded in the late 1960s by Sweeney's Men. Seán O'Dwyer's concertina playing may be heard on a Free Reed anthology of Irish concertina players, Irish Traditional Concertina Styles.

DISCOGRAPHY

This is a listing of a number of commercially-recorded tinwhistle performances encompassing a wide range of ability, repertoire, and style. You can find them at Irish import stores, record distributors via mail-order, or the companies that produced them, though some may be out-of-print. Only four albums have so far been devoted entirely to the tinwhistle (#1-4), and some ave only one track of solo whistle playing. Ensembles such as the Chieftains, Bothy Band, Boys of the Lough, Na Filí, Planxty, Ceoltóirí Laighean, Ceoltóirí Cualann, etc. use one or more whistles throughout the course of an album, and records by these groups often contain some tinwhistle gems that flash by quickly and unexpectedly.

This listing gives performances that are worthwhile listening to, whether you like the style or player. I never met a musician who I wasn't able to learn something from, even if it was what not to do. These selections give an idea of what other people do with the instrument.

The album title is given first; if the tinwhistle player is a featured or solo performer throughout the album, that is the name that follows the album title. Otherwise, the tinwhistle player's name is prefaced by this sign: w/.

1. Tinwhistles, Paddy Moloney & Seán Potts. Claddagh CC15.

2. Tom McHaile, Tom McHaile. Outlet OLP1001.

3. Donncha Ó Brían, Donncha Ó Brían. Gael Linn CEF083.

4. Mary Bergin, Mary Bergin. Shanachie SH79006.

5. Lord Mayo, Le Chéile w/ P.J. Crotty. Inchecronin 7424.

6. Arís!, Le Chéile w/ P.J. Crotty. Inchecronin 7423.

7. De Danann, De Danann w/ Frank Gavin. Polydor 2904.

8. Frank Gavin & Alec Finn w/ Frank Gavin. Shanachie SH29008.

9. Chieftains 3, Chieftains w/ Seán Potts. Claddagh CC10.

10. The Breeze from Erin, various artists w/ Willie Clancy, Festy Conlan, Eddie Corcoran, Seamus Tansey. Topic 12T184.

11. The Minstrel from Clare, Willie Clancy. Topic 12T175.

12. Seoda Ceoil #1, various artists w/ Willie Clancy. Gael-Linn CEF018.

13. Paddy Keenan, various artists w/ Paddy & Tom Keenan. Gael-Linn CEF045.

14. Grand Airs from Connemara, various artists w/ Festy Conlan. Topic 12T177.

15. More Grand Airs from Connemara, various artists w/ Festy Conlan. Topic 12T202.

16. An Irish Jubilee, Cathal McConnell. Topic 12T290.

17. On Lough Erne's Shore, Cathal McConnell. Topic 12T377.

18. A Kindly Welcome, Na Filí w/ Tom Barry. Dolphin DOL1008.

19. From the Homes of Ireland, various artists w/ Deirdre Collis. Comhaltas Ceoltóirí Éireann CL8.

20. The Home I Left Behind, various artists w/ Deirdre Collis & Donal de Barra. Comhaltas Ceoltóirí Éireann CL9.

21. Comhaltas Champions on Tour, various artists w/ Anne Sheehy & Nick McAuliffe. Comhaltas Ceoltóirí Éireann CL11.
22. The Irish Pipes of Finbar Furey, Finbar Furey. Nonesuch H-72048.
23. Irish Pipe Music, Finbar Furey. Nonesuch H-72059.
24. The Russell Family, Miko & Gus Russell. Topic 12TS251.
25. Traditional Country Music from County Clare, Miko Russell. Free Reed FRR004.
26. The Bonny Bunch of Roses, Seamus Ennis. Tradition TLP1013.
27. Seamus Ennis, Seamus Ennis. Leader LEA2003.
28. Seamus Tansey, Seamus Tansey & Eddie Corcoran. Leader LEA2005.
29. Music from Coleman Country, various artists w/ Jim Donaghue. Leader LEA2044.
30. Bonnie Kate, various artists w/ Mary Bergin. Comhaltas Ceoltóirí Éireann CL2.
31. Darby's Farewell, Josie McDermott. Topic 12T325.
32. The Eagle's Whistle, Michael Tubridy. Claddagh CC27.
33. Joe & Antoinette McKenna, Joe McKenna. Shanachie SH29011.
34. Dan Sullivan's Shamrock Band, Dan Sullivan's Shamrock Band w/ Dan Moroney. Topic 12T366.

****Recordings by L.E. McCullough****

Hollow Poplar, various artists w/ L.E. McCullough. Log Cabin 8003.

Ladies on the Flatboat, various artists w/ L.E. McCullough. Log Cabin 8004.

Second Annual Smoky City Folk Festival, various artists w/ L.E. McCullough. Wildebeest WB001.

The Ghost of His Former Self, Devilish Merry w/ L.E. McCullough. Wildebeest WB002. WB002.

two forthcoming albums from Rounder Records: The Music of Ed Reavy

Irish-American Flute & Tinwhistle Players

L.E. McCULLOUGH was born in Speedway, Indiana, the
year Troy Ruttman won the Indy 500. An accomplished
performer in several contemporary musical idioms, he
became involved in Irish music while living in Ireland
during 1971-1972 and quickly achieved a substantial
reputation as a collector, scholar, and performer of
of Irish music. He has won several prizes in Irish
music competitions (including the 1975 All-Ireland
Senior Tinwhistle Contest), has published numerous
articles in leading academic and popular journals,
and has produced radio programs, records, and video-
tapes on aspects of folk music. His Ph.D. in ethno-
musicology from the University of Pittsburgh in 1978
is the first Ph.D. dissertation ever written on Irish
music in Ireland or America. Currently residing in
Pittsburgh, he is the director of the Pennsylvania
Folk Music Research Institute and does freelance
music, writing, folk arts consulting, and cat ranching.

NOTES

NOTES

NOTES

NOTES

NOTES

NOTES

NOTES

NOTES